Of the Sea:

An anthology of prose and poetry

Aidan Parr

Of the Sea: an anthology of prose and poetry

ISBN-13:
9781795367011

This publication is available in paper and electronic formats.

Contents

Forward

This is my first attempt at an anthology and contains a mixture of prose and poetry I've written in the past few years.

Most of it is about people who are sad, lonely, funny, odd, angry, sweary and eccentric. I also love the sea and much of that comes out in my work, particularly in my poems.

I hope you enjoy it!

I've always wanted to write, but life has always presented me with obstacles: we all have to make a living to pay the rent, eat and have some leisure time. That leaves a lot less time for writing.

I was lucky enough to meet some supportive people in March 2017 who encouraged me to start. Thanks must go to them- you know who you are and I can't begin to get across how grateful I am.

I didn't really need much more encouragement...

Thanks must also go to Phil Pidluznyj and Mark Barry, who run the 'Creative Writing & Self-Publishing' course at Nottingham College. I've become a better writer and had opportunities to get my work published and read it out at events in Nottingham because of them.

Cheers to 'The Snug' writing group in Beeston for being so supportive and critical of what I write. Listening to what you write in turn is always a treat and has inspired me to want to know more.

The Nottingham Writers' Studio also deserve praise and not just because they awarded me 'Blogger of the Year' for my website, 'A Bloke

Dyslexic', in 2018, although I am probably biased!

There have been opportunities at NWS to learn more about verse, fiction and non-fiction have made me a better poet, too. I have gone from being purely a prose writer to someone who also enjoys writing poems, albeit with a lot to learn.

I am fortunate to have inherited an interest in writing from my Mum, Una Parr. Many of you will be aware that I self-published her collection of poems, 'Life, Nature and the Spirit' in 2018. She was quite shy about what she'd written and hid her work, but was delighted I'd made a book for her. Sadly, she never got the opportunity to learn more and was never encouraged.

If you do write on the quiet, go and attend a class or a writing group. I don't think you'll be sorry!

Thanks must also go, yet again, to Lucy Kong Creative for the beautiful cover and Victoria McDonagh for proof-reading, editing and being critical in the best sense of the word, as usual!

There's a novel in the works from me, too. After that, who knows?

Aidan Parr

March 2019

Poetry

St. Vitus Dance

It's a St. Vitus dance of adolescence,

Too much energy unchallenged.

Unencouraged.

No school of worth,

No parent of talent,

Sliding into a mediocre life:

Drugs, drink, sex.

Casual violence.

Then children of their own.

No plan, no joy, a stop on 'fun',

Not yet developed,

They develop the next to come,

Feeling like a curse unwanted,

Down the worst path straight from conception.

There's no hero,

No saviour,

There's nothing.

In their turn it's a St. Vitus dance of adolescence,

Too much energy unchallenged.

Unencouraged.

No school of worth,

No parent of talent,

Sliding into a mediocre life:

Drugs, drink, sex.

Casual violence.

Then children of their own.

No plan, no joy, a stop on 'fun',

Not yet developed,

They develop the next to come,

Feeling like a curse unwanted,

Down the worst path straight from conception.

Down and down we all go...

There's no hero,

No saviour,

There's nothing.

Nothing.

Pity Me

Pity me, pity me, pity me,

People are so mean to me.

Pity me, pity me, pity me,

The world is hard on me.

Pity me, pity me, pity me,

Friends desert me.

Pity me, pity me, pity me,

My family do not love me.

Pity me, pity me, pity me,

Life is unkind to me.

Pity me, pity me, pity me,

My workmates make fun of me.

Pity me, pity me, pity me,

The people I desire don't see me.

Pity me, pity me, pity me,

My boss does not like me.

Pity me, pity me, pity me,

The man last week who talked for a while now

ignores me.

Pity me, pity me, pity me,

The woman at the bus stop avoids me.

Pity me, pity me, pity me,

My disability defines me.

Pity me, pity me, pity me,

Opportunities blind me.

Pity me, pity me, pity me,

Above all else pity me.

Pity me, pity me, pity me,

Above all else pity me.

This poem previously appeared in the 'Bright Sparks'

anthology.

Young Chick Hates Old Bird (and vice-versa)

You hate me, young chick:

I am grey and slow and self-important.

Arrogant.

I hate you too, young chick:

You have possibilities.

You waste them in so many ways.

You are original…

Or so you think!

I cringe silently about 'How you will change the world'

As you're dart here and there and back again.

I tried that once.

It changed me.

Into…

What you see before you.

Grey:

Slow and thoughtful and chewing on the past

and my own future,

I still don't 'get it' and I never will.

Self-important:

My zest, the desire to share, to share and to

share, all shame diminished,

The wonders done, the wonders now and the

wonders that are yet to come.

Arrogant:

The excitement of sharing, sharing, sharing and

sharing again.

I can't help it.

Some learning, from you, too.

Why not?

You astound me and make me feel unworthy.

I know, see, feel, and understand (but so weakly)

And there are not enough hours

To show you, talk to you, understand you,

Or even complete myself.

You have so much talent and so much time...

I think I hate you more.

A Poetic End

Dying piece by piece,

A little niggle here, then there, as it spreads

everywhere.

She lies there.

She forgets. She forgets. She forgets.

Forgets her music. Forgets her children. Forgets

her life.

Poems are constant,

Although she never remembers the reading.

Over and over the old favourites,

Hour after hour in delight and rapture.

Always beginning with Yeats,

Always ending with

'When You Are Old'.

We in turn laugh and cry and struggle,

She has the better part.

Surrounded by beauty and rhythmic dancing,

Hope, struggle and meaning.

What a precious way to leave this tawdry world.

Lifted by care and love,

But most of all on the wings of poetry.

Spring at Dusk

The chill drives away the sun and its heat,
Darkness descends as the light slowly stills,
Intense floral perfumes collide and meet,
Ecstasy of scent, my joyous heart fills.

The throngs of birds fill the dusk with singing,
Calling their mates or challenge to battle,
Beauty, strength, cruel, savage blood ringing,
Ending harsh winter, signs of renewal.

I sit in the night-time filled with wonder
Wild delights of Creation I ponder.

You've Never…

Cold snap burning on your face, hands, those
eyes,
Mists of wonder, azure above, the clouds,
You've never seen the greatness in the skies,
Your feet, sight, your being, down in the crowds.

You've never let your inner vision fly,
That mind always chained to clods of the earth,
Never asking, believing, wondered 'Why?'
Ever seeking sameness from days of birth.

Dead from your first breath of life sans meaning,
Rewarded with rags, basest coins, gleaming.

At Dunwich

Dunwich: Sic transit gloria mundi,
Seven church bells toll beneath wave and storm,
From the ocean's roar, the people did flee,
A busy port, now no purpose or form.

Rival to London, city of riches,
The monastic ruin broods on the hill,
Each year that passes, the tide encroaches,
All that remains: wind, sand, bleakness and chill.

Oh foolish man you fight to build a wall,
The eternal sea comes to take you all.

Evanescence

Like the morning mist we come and we go,

Our proudest vanity hammered by time,

Ever tales of triumph, defeat and woe,

Always ridiculous, errant, sublime.

Your vanity shrieks upon their regard,

Emptiness lasts but a generation,

Against vanity, celebrity guard,

They are a cancer, a suppuration.

Life is a void filled with lines of untruth,

Give in to wonder and purpose anew.

The Single Shoe

The single shoe, tattered and worn lies there,

In the empty room, your favourite spot,

Your ghost of a presence everywhere,

Your life full of living ends up in rot.

All is removed save the silent voices,

Laughter, poesy, rhymes, riddles recited,

Anger, resentment, decisions, choices,

Echo with small cries, joyous, excited.

This house is no place without your warm light,

No home, no hearth: cast out, darkness, the

night.

The Storm

The sea beyond the dunes gathers,

Its force begins so slow,

From blue, then grey, its strength matters,

The wind, once soft, now blows.

A shriek, a howl, intense, powers

A maelstrom hurling fast,

The waves that crash the shore for hours,

Fierceness, the ocean vast.

Batters the headland in its might,

Flotsam, jetsam, wreckage,

Driving the day to savage night,

No hope of anchorage.

The timbers rattle, mainsail flies,

Steerage against the swell,

This is the storm that takes their lives,

This is the storm from hell.

Torrents of water blinding eyes,

A surge men bringing low,

Turmoil full of desperate cries,

Swept away by the flow.

Morning comes shining, depths so calm,

The wails of the women.

No peace, no succour and no balm,

Their faces are ashen.

Scrape that Wall: a villanelle

Scrape that wall, break through, break out, all
mettle,
Your nails, fingers, hands, your teeth, til they
bleed,
Like a dog claws the door, its rage feral.

Yelling you want, the longing, terrible,
Screaming for freedom, they'll pay you no heed,
Scrape that wall, break through, break out, all
mettle.

Don't stop, no resting, show them your nettle,
Show them contempt, dislike, anger, don't plead,
Like a dog claws the door, its rage feral.

Learn their ways, learn where they're weak, be
brutal,
Faux kindness, lures, pretended and parried,

Scrape that wall, break through, break out, all
mettle.

Never be fooled by their words genial,
The day you're not charmed you'll be pilloried,
Like a dog claws the door, its rage feral.

Sometimes you're lonely, sometimes you're
mournful,
Sometimes dead to the world but not buried,
Scrape that wall, break through, break out, all
mettle,
Like a dog claws the door, its rage feral.

Devilish Rhythm and Heavenly Blues

You stand, you sway, you tap your feet,

You smile, you nod, you're so complete,

The singer groans about his hard times,

Something so joyous in that beat,

Infectious movement, it's so sweet.

Up it rises to your knees,

The diva begs, yells and pleads,

Sold her soul to make these rhymes,

Hits those strings, effortlessly,

Sings those words with passion and ease.

The tempo gets into your hips,

He struts, suggests, a solo rips,

New words, old tales he got from Nick,

They're in your ears, they're on your lips,

It makes you move, groove and dip.

The downbeat moves into your chest,

Moving closely with all the rest,

Dancing freely to the Devil's songs,

You move, in chains, at his behest,

The music takes you, hypnotic caress.

Now the rhythm's in your head,

The body moving, eyes are dead,

No more thoughts, little care,

Alternative thinking and doubts have fled,

Enthralled, happy, to hell you're led.

You raise your hands up to the sky,

Pointing at heaven but don't know why,

Looking empty at the blues,

There's other things to gratify,

Empty promises or...

Just. Pure. Lies.

This poem previously appeared in the 'Pyrography' anthology.

Like Phosphorous Lighting

I burn for you like phosphorous lighting,

Quenched in those tears, doused in my heart's

thick red,

Fire never goes out, blazes brightening.

The years pass by, the yearnings frightening,

Lifeless and poisoned and so much unsaid,

I burn for you like phosphorous lighting.

Longing for an end, for a darkening,

Dying a thousand and more instead,

Fire never goes out, blazes brightening.

A shell of a man waiting for firing,

Discarded, unstable, ageing warhead,

I burn for you like phosphorous lighting.

I greet and I smile, cursing the watching,

Explosions of wanting, the lust in my head,

Fire never goes out, blazes brightening.

My longing for you, hell of my making,
If you knew you'd reject, my love misread,
I burn for you like phosphorous lighting,
Fire never goes out, blazes brightening.

This poem previously appeared in the 'Pyrography'
anthology.

The Meat Machine Roasting

I'm the meat machine that you manage,

I'm the robot that you wield,

I'm the nothing on the scrap heap,

I'm the memory of no-one,

I'm in a hole and six feet down.

I'm the one with no dignity,

I'm the one you hold in contempt,

I'm the homeless living rough,

I'm the addict shaking with need,

I'm the illegal, so phone the police.

I'm the one who can't fit in,

I'm the one with odd ideas,

I'm the one in the wheelchair,

I'm the one you respond to with jeers,

I'm the one at the end of your fist.

I'm the one who's old and lonely,

I'm the one who desires but fears,

I'm the one who'll end up in hellfire,

I'm the sinner, the apostate,

I'm the meat machine roasting.

I'm the one with my own ambitions,

I'm the one with my own set of joys,

I'm the one who loves and is loved,

I'm the one who sets the world alight,

I'm the one who can lessen a burden.

I'm the one who should be cherished.

This poem previously appeared in the 'Pyrography' anthology.

I Got These Blues

I got these blues that are creeping up on me.

I got these blues, I think I need a tonic.

I got these downers they're almost chronic

I'm histrionic, surrounded like quadraphonic

Sometimes ironic, soporific, dulled a la narcotics,

exaggerated and tragi-comic.

I got these blues that are leeching off me.

In the morning, they're growing on me.

Through the day, it sounds lunatic.

Mostly feel sceptic, but completely spasmodic

Makes me feel like a dipstick

A life that is slapstick, thoughts that are toxic

Suspended in traffic, insufficiently stoic.

Like weeds that should be protozoic.

The only cure is you to fix these blues.

The cure is you, how about we frolic?

I get so cheered it's episodic, always

erotic, sometimes erratic, eccentric and spastic

Like we're made of elastic, delicious and manic

Communion mystic, relativistic

Mind-blowing and cosmic.

You fix those blues that live in me.

Damp Grass, Wet Feet

The Garden still stands

Filled with glory and beauty

The serpent told his story

Temptation original

Damp grass wet feet the Apple

In Nature's delight

The animals and mankind

In full harmony

The sounding of the calling

Their delights primordial

Conceived in a day

Man and woman together

Then a lesson from wisdom

Become like a God knowing

Good and evil have meaning

Hiding from the storm

Naked shame and denial

The man now blaming

The woman she made me eat

Out of Eden and exiled

Now knowing allure

Embroiled and cruel and savage

Now realising

Knowledge and desiring home

Damp grass wet feet and tortured

This poem previously appeared in the 'Pyrography' anthology.

Juncture

In Spring there is change

Gentle soft breezes blowing

My world awakens

For you are with me my love

Your gentle touch is a balm

The burning sun high

The scent of flowers in bloom

My heart turns colder

The days are long and tiresome

For you have gone from my life

Autumn now calling

The stench of damp and wet leaves

My tears have fallen

The dark grey skies oppress me

Low in spirit and in life

The frosty chill now

The blue skies and sun return

I ache with cold and absence

Dark bitterness inside me

My yearning is not returned

This poem previously appeared in the 'Pyrography'
anthology.

Above, Below, the Sea

Swells dark, swells light, changes and churns
abound,
Above the black, a maw of hell reigns free,
Below blazes heaven's brightness around,
Chaos, order, above, below, the sea.

Salt and water in movement, contingent,
Tides ebbing and flowing contained by time,
Their battles millennial and ancient,
Beginning to end, warfare maritime.

Storm clouds swooping down to battle their foe,
Sunlight's bright swords pierce the veil slicing
through,
Incandescence shining, darkness cut low,
Shadows smothering, brilliance withdrew.

And so I watch the mighty ocean raw,
I am tiny. Unimportant. In awe.

This poem previously appeared in the 'Bright Sparks' anthology.

Haiku

Trump puts the prayer
In the crumbling Wailing Wall,
Love note to himself.

Dementia taxed,
Parents will fade to nothing
Their heirs are paupers.

Bombers of children,
Anger denies innocence,
Joy snuffed out by rage.

A riot of green,
Perfume and colour is bliss,
Birdsong soothes the soul.

Dementia Dad,
Agitation rules him now,

Driven empty tasks.

Books impart wisdom.

Challenge your thinking today.

Reading expands you.

Refusal is all.

All sense is lost forever,

You love them much less.

They wish partition,

I ask for reasons and proof,

"We're British," they say.

Bawls like a baby,

Dead cat syrup on his head,

President Trump now.

Ant going to work,

Shiny car and gleaming teeth,

Hate festers inside.

Your children are fools

Understanding nothing now.

All led by the nose.

Social media:

Narcissus is put to shame.

Look at me now. Now!

Once honourable,

Now less, but proud. Idiots!

The world keeps changing.

She prays to her God

For release and for comfort,

Nothing changes there.

Cold. Calculating.

No love inside or on show,

You are dead really.

One laughs, the other

Sits and mopes in petulance,

I choose the former.

I watch the ocean:

Her moods, her capriciousness,

Still, always entranced.

Prose

Of the Sea

"If the rain comes…" said my Uncle.

"What do you mean?" replied Mum. We were in Ireland. It had rained solidly for a week.

"Real rain. Wet rain. Not that dry stuff ye have over there, Maggie."

"'Dry rain?' Ye've reminded me Seamus why I went off to England to get away from here."

'Here' was a small farm in the north-west of Ireland. Twenty acres of grass, a small herd of cows and nothing else. It was ten miles from Achill Island and felt the full force of the Atlantic all year round. Spring was wet, but nice, summer was just wet, autumn was wet and windy and winter was wet, windy and not nice at all.

My Aunt Bridget summed it up well: "It rains and it rains, but it's worse in the Summer, because the days are longer."

"Arra, get away with ye!" said Seamus. "All that fancy pants ways. Foreign nonsense. What's wrong with the way things are? Pretending they put a man on the moon. All Hollywood filums. All on the same stage!"

Mum rolled her eyes. It was the same old Seamus. His battered 1936 astronomy book would come out next. Anxious to change the subject, Mum turned back to Seamus. "How's Mammy?"

Seamus' face softened. "Much the same. Complains. Likes the attention. Sometimes not with us at all. Sometimes sharp as a tack. She'll be pleased to see you, Maggie."

"And me to see her, Seamus."

We'd gone to Ireland to see Grandma Lynch, but the care home staff would not let anyone near her. I'd heard Mum complain that they especially wanted to keep her away.

"I had the cheek to move away! And marry an Englishman. No-one from around here will ever forgive that!"

It was probably true. Dad did come with Mum for holidays. He was a quiet man who couldn't cope with his talkative in-laws. In the end it was convenient to say that he was 'busy with work'. Mum's family and neighbours admired hard workers, so that gave Dad a way out.

I make it sound like they were bad people. But they weren't. Mum's family were complex, moody, funny, sarcastic, argumentative and affectionate.

They were descendants of fisherman who plied their trade out in the seas around the coast of County Mayo. They passed down myths of terrible nights where men died, wives were widowed and children orphaned when the women died of grief.

It was all told with a twinkle in the eye, each speaker trying to outdo each other in sensational, tall tales.

Mum's family were like the sea. No, they were the sea. The storms, troughs, depressions, bleakness, stillness, sunny joys, wildness and calms were part of them. They were the sea and the sea was them. Everything was felt fully. It was a huge contrast to my normal home life that was calm, repressed and very English.

At night, everyone would be around the table. There would be chat, debate and arguments. It was seldom that family members took offence, although Uncle Joe's famed forty mile drive to Westport 'to buy fish' had gone into family folklore. He'd got into a terrible argument with Mum about women's rights. 'Buying fish' equated to 'not murdering each other'. Then it was all forgotten the next day.

Differences came and went, like the tide. It was just like writing names or building sandcastles at the beach. You built it up and the sea smoothed it away or knocked it down. Nothing remained but the 'now'.

On the best nights, the poitín would come out and everyone would sing and play. Neighbours would were made welcome. My Mum was a surprisingly good singer, but Seamus was the best accordion player. They often sang together and everyone else joined in the chorus. Even me, so self-conscious, would join in, especially after a thimble or two of moonshine.

Seamus was a champion piss-taker and would often try to put me on the spot. I hated him sometimes but later I grew to have a similar outlook on life. It was the fashion for twelve year olds at the time to have long hair. When we'd arrived Seamus peered myopically at me saying "And how's herself?"

Everyone else laughed.

"Leave him be, Seamus, he's only a boy!" Uncle Joe said. But Seamus would continue the mockery.

"But look at him! Ye couldn't tell if he was a boy or a girl…"

He'd eventually stop. Eventually.

It had taken a few hours to tune into how everyone talked. Mum's voice would go from a polite Anglo-Irish accent to full-blown Mayo twang in seconds leaving me bewildered. I'm sure they were all convinced I was 'a bit slow'. English was strangely mixed with Gaelic to make me more confused.

Uncle Joe would ask 'Dún an doras' and expect me to understand. Mum would take pity on me.

"Uncle Joe wants you to shut the door, Tom." Uncle Joe would occasionally call me 'a spalpeen' or 'a little curraghbuck' if he thought I was being cheeky. Seamus would refer to me as 'the puss dhtuggairt' if I was sulky.

I had to get used to being called 'Tam' and my corrections were politely ignored. Sometimes I was 'that little omethain' if I was too quiet and shy, but Mum, like the tigress, would soon savage anyone who said things to hurt. Mockery was allowed and a family tradition, but respect was enforced, usually by the women. You could tease children, but not too much.

The days were spent trudging round fields in the rain. Normally on my own. It sounds terrible but I enjoyed it. The wild weather, the endless rain, the greenness of it all. I'd come back soaked from head to sodden feet and they'd all smile at me as if I learnt a great secret. They never let on what it was, but I was at peace there and I've never found it anywhere else.

We were finally allowed to see Grandma. Mum, me and Uncle Joe set off to the care home. It was an old estate house built by an Anglo-Irish family in the 17th Century, with granite walls, high ceilings and huge fireplaces.

The nun welcomed Joe warmly, but ignored Mum. Mum's face was bleak as she tried not to get angry at the deliberate slur. The woman turned to me with a welcoming smile: "Is this one of your sons, Joe?"

Her face fell as Joe explained, "No, he's Maggie's. Can't you see it in him?"

After that I was ignored too.

Grandma was in a small room in the attic space. It was clean and functional with a crucifix on the wall, statue of the Virgin Mary and rosary beads. It wasn't anything like the Grandma Lynch I knew who lived in chaos with books, newspapers and the 'Sacred Heart Messenger' piled high.

Grandma lay there, tiny in the bed, the yellowing flesh on her face stuck to her skull. But when she saw us, she gave a radiant smile, delighted to see her daughter. And quite pleased to see me too.

"Maggie! Ye finally got around to coming then! And you brought Tam too! Why lookut! Almost a man and the spit of you."

Mum and I took turns to give her a kiss. Then it was Mum and Grandma chatting away, ten to the dozen for the next hour. I sat there, politely bored.

They went through what I'd nicknamed 'The Litany of the Dead': who'd died, what they died of, how long it took and 'wasn't it an awful world we lived in with all these fine people dying on us'. Cancers, tumours, peculiar growths and hideously delicate operations were discussed with great gusto.

I cringed when Grandma described in great detail where one neighbour had 'had almost his entire stomach taken out' and 'could only live on chicken'.

Uncle Joe, seeing my revulsion, gave a little cough and rolled his eyes at me when I looked. We both tried to suppress smiles, but he kept grinning and winking at me, until I let out an involuntary snort of laughter.

"Something funny, Tom?" asked Mum.

I tried to look innocent. "No, I just need a drink of water."

Mum gave a smile herself. "Off you go. Go and get a drink of water. Take your uncle with you. Keep him out of the pub!"

We didn't need to be told twice. We were soon down the stairs and out the front door.

"What a good idea," Joe said. "I could murther a pint 'a stout. How about you, Tam?"

"I don't think I'm allowed..."

"Stuff an' nonsense! If I say ye'll have a pint, ye'll have a pint. No, come on! We've both got a powerful thirst from listenin' to the women talk about death and operations."

So we walked the half mile down the 'The Broken Jug'. The walls were black from a peat fire that gave off a sweet, smoky smell. It was a rough-looking place with a few old farmers propping up the bar or leaned back in their chairs.

The lady behind the bar greeted us. "Joe! How are ye?"

My uncle smiled back. "Not so bad, Siobhan. A pint for me and a glass of stout for the young man."

She looked at me. "And who is this?"

"Tam. Maggie's youngest."

She paused and then laughed. "I should have known! That hair! Black as night! And those green-grey-blue eyes. Who could doubt?"

"He's the very same, indeed. Now, the stout...?" Uncle Joe nodded at the hand-pump.

"Ah! Of course. I shall admire the young man later!"

'Tam the slow' took over. I just blushed and looked at the floor.

"He'll have to beat the girls off with a stick in a few years, won't he Siobhan?"

They both laughed again at my discomfort.

"I'll bring the stout over when it's ready..."

I headed for the corner seat, well away from anyone else, Joe following. "There's no sense in being all shy when a woman thinks you're handsome, Tam."

I flushed red again. "I'm not used to people saying those things about me."

"Aska braw! Round here if we like what we see, we say it. Too used to English ways, Tam. You're a dacent looking boy and you'll be a dacent looking man. Better get used to it!"

65

Joe spoke again. "Your mother was the prettiest girl from around these parts, Tam. She had many a young man come calling. Some to woo her and some to just get in her knickers. De ye understand?"

I was mortified but nodded glumly.

"Sometimes beauty is a curse. Maggie never had the chance here to be herself. It was her looks people always noticed. Her brains came second to her beauty."

I nodded again. Why was he saying this?

"When you're older, ye'll have many a pretty girl chasing after ye too, Tam. Remember that it's your looks," he chuckled, "your beauty they'll be after. All with the glad eye. Remember that, won't ye?"

"Yes, Uncle Joe," I hoped he'd change the subject. To my relief Siobhan came with the Guinness. Joe nodded his thanks and I looked at the table.

He took a good quaff and swallowed with a little moan. "Ah, that's the stuff!"

I followed suit and took a mouthful. It was without doubt the most disgusting thing I'd ever tasted. I coughed as I tried to swallow and it went down the wrong hole.

The whole pub laughed at my discomfort as stout came out my nose and mouth as I choked. Joe thumped me on the back and Siobhan quickly arrived with a cloth to wipe my face with.

"First Guinness?" shouted a red-faced farmer, all tweed and the scent of rotting hay.

"'Tis indeed!" replied Joe and the whole pub took to laughing at me again.

It was at that point Mum walked through the door...

The sea was very stormy that night and unsettled for days.

This story previously appeared in the 'Bright Sparks' anthology.

Led by Donkeys

1918 was the centenary of the end of the First World War. In November of that year, the guns went quiet and the fire between the Allies and the Central Powers ceased. The 'War to End All Wars' ended in Europe, at least for twenty years.

It's an anniversary that seems to mean so much to some and nothing to others. The latter ignore the consequences of that first industrial war at their peril: the mass slaughter, the sundering of empires, the creation of new nation-states and the stoking of resentment that eventually led to the Second World War.

Like many, I have an ancestor who fought in the trenches. Gunner George was wounded three times. It was on his first convalescence in Derbyshire that he met the woman who would become his wife and who was my grandmother.

We have little to show for him. A few worn ribbons and a medal, ironically titled '1914-1919 – The Battle to Save Civilisation'. Little did anyone know that twenty years later, war would again be declared to save us from a far more insidious political creed.

One postcard tells his then wife to 'not worry, it's only a small thing'. A 'Blighty' as he termed it. A chance to be sent home for a short while. His modesty seems to outweigh even his bravery. Later, another wound.

The generals and the leaders were safe: far behind the horrors of trench warfare. The phrase 'Lions led by donkeys' is apocryphal, but it does tell some truth. The soldiers fought and died or were maimed because their leaders made series after series of foolish decisions.

When George was discharged, it was back to the usual world of the early twentieth century: casual labour and poor wages. We only know that he suffered from ill-health and eventually lost his regular job. So much for a 'land fit for heroes'?

Nine years later, he was out of work, married with two small children and another on the way. He drowned in a terrible accident on the Derwent trying to make a living. The child on the way, only a month-old collections of cells was my father.

The effects are long-term. A wife with no husband to provide, working at several jobs to keep the family going, a boy and a girl with no father and another boy, yet to be born, who never got to know his father at all. It is a family traumatised.

Today we would probably say that my grandmother had post-traumatic stress disorder.

Family legend tells that my grandmother told the army representative to 'get stuffed' when they wanted to give George a military salute at his grave, guns blazing, but would not volunteer anything material or financial to support his wife or children. The family were left to get on with it, through the Great Depression of the 1930s and then a return to war.

All because the leaders, in wartime and in peacetime are donkeys. As in warfare, as in peace.

We now in the twenty-first century make one of the most profound decisions about our nation's future. The referendum of 2016 was decided by the public based on the lies and the braying of our political leaders.

Many of us are now aware that what was offered by the champions of Brexit was fuelled by untruths and self-interest. They will prosper and we will suffer.

Why are always content to be led by donkeys?

This article previously appeared in the 'Pyrography' anthology.

Just Like That...

I once met a man who had been at Porton Down. Steve had been conscripted into the army in the 1950's. One day he and his squad were ordered into a room with no windows. The door was closed.

Then they were exposed to nerve agents.

No one ever admitted responsibility for doing this to Steve or any of the others who were deliberately exposed to sarin and other poisonous gases. They never got compensation.

I met Steve when he was in his seventies. A friendly, but highly strung man with a curious tremor. As he told me about his life, his hands constantly moved up and down. I saw this movement and it suddenly came to me, "Tommy Cooper – 'Just like that'".

For fifty years Steve had lived his life ("Just like that").

Discharged from the army with ill-health ("Just like that").

Permanently disabled ("Just like that").

Tried to live a 'normal' life ("Just like that").

Courted his girlfriend ("Just like that").

Got married ("Just like that").

His wife gave birth to a son ("Just like that").

And then a few more kids ("Just like that").

He found it hard to get a permanent job ("Just like that").

Retired early with a basic pension ("Just like that").

His wife got dementia ("Just like that").

And then she died ("Just like that").

He lived a lonely life on his own ("Just like that").

"Just like that". "Just like that". "Just like that".
"Just like that". "Just like that". "Just like that".
"Just like that". "Just like that". "Just like that".
"Just like that". "Just like that". "Just like that".
"Just like that". "Just like that". "Just like that".

Every minute of every day, for the rest of his life.

"Just like that".

Christmas Gifts

"Hello darling! Did you have a lovely Christmas? Don't rush off I haven't seen you in ages, you always have things to do!

"Ours was just perfect, I went to the Midnight Service and got up early to start Christmas dinner. I had far too many guests as usual but you know how it is with me, can't resist inviting people. The minister didn't come. I suppose he's got his own family to be with, but it would be such a coup for me to get him to our Christmas dinners. He'd never refuse again!

"Before dinner we delivered the Christmas presents to those poor, poor people still in the hospital. I must have spent a small fortune on wrapping paper, only the best you know. It gets dearer every year the best gift-wrap but I do think it's important not to skimp. I always look

forward to seeing their little faces light up –
they've got no-one you know and it cheers me
up to give them some Christmas cheer.

"What was in the wrapping paper? Darling, as if
that's important! It's the giving you see, the
giving that's important. Still we did put some
nice things in there, you know. The usual sort of
essential knick-knacks: pot-pourri, toothpaste,
toothbrush, a flannel, and some scented soaps.
They smelt beautiful!

"I couldn't bear the idea that they couldn't be
clean for a change and have something lovely to
smell at this time of year. It's nice for them to
see that at least I care about them, especially if
no-one else does. And the girls of course, how
would I get all my good work done without
them?

"Mind you, sometimes I don't know why we bother to be honest. Many seemed delighted when we gave them a gift but they soon lost interest after they opened it. Don't they know how much work we put into to giving them a present?

"One man cried. I felt so embarrassed; he seemed to be so grateful. I suppose when he told us to go away it was because he was embarrassed too. The nurses closed the curtains around his bed and they wouldn't let us back. The poor dear, I expect he was feeling exhausted. These invalids tire so easily.

"Of course men don't mind scented things! My husband always used to like the house smelling nice. He was a proper gentleman, you know, God rest his soul. He would have never taken against me in any of my charity work at Christmas. He was a rock, you know? I keep busy helping people now, that's what keeps me going.

"Some must have been very ill, there was so much sneezing! One of the nurses suggested that some people have an allergy to perfume! Silly girl, I've been doing this for years and no-one ever complains. They should be more concerned about treating those poor patients than talking to me about allergies. I've never had an allergy in my life... still, perhaps it was nice of them to ask, in case I did have a problem.

"When I went back the next week, none of my presents were there. I suppose the nurses might have tidied them away for when these unfortunates go home. If some of them do go home. I'm not sure they are all... all there, if you understand me.

"When they do go home, I'm sure I and the girls will be the first to volunteer to give some practical help. Our Shake 'n' Vac is at the ready!

"We're already planning a lovely Easter gift for the rest of them who don't."

An Italian Story

'Thud!' went the dart into the picture on the wall.

"I have done alright for myself!" thought Giovanni. And indeed he had.

But every so often, the mood would come upon him and several times a year "that bloody picture" would come out. And he'd throw darts at it.

The other picture on the wall was of himself, taken many years ago, when he was twenty. His first trip to England, an awkward Italian exchange student, just a shy boy really. He could remember the clumsiness, his way of becoming embarrassed over everything and nothing. So long ago, but he still remembered so clearly.

That was the exchange holiday when he realised he could escape. Born of a poor Italian family, but cursed with that ancestral name. The children at his school tormented him: the awkward, shy child with his heart on his sleeve, a complete contrast to his famous great, great, great grandfather, the statesmen and great unifier.

He threw another dart, another 'Thud' and remembered the taunting.

In England, no one recognised the name, except for occasional comments about 'biscuits with dead flies in them'. It took him years to get the joke and he still didn't think it was funny. He liked the English but he didn't think he'd ever quite understand them.

However, the holiday stuck with him, the freedom of being unknown and with no expectations. Against the protests of his family, he went travelling. There would be no university and half-hearted attempts at diplomatic studies that his family could ill-afford.

Round Europe he went and eventually found himself in London. Short of cash and with no desire to go home, he applied for a job in a printers. He recalled the dirty office, papers piled everywhere and the old man, working all alone, with a constant cigarette hanging out of his mouth as he coughed and spluttered what he expected the young Giovanni to do.

The place was horrifying, but money is money and Giovanni started, printing the fliers, loading the van and delivering thousands and soon millions of flyers advertising sales, diets, canine beauticians and mobile hairdressers. He found he enjoyed the physical hard work and his shyness disappeared the more he interacted with ordinary English people.

The old man, the owner, took a shine to Giovanni and started to show how the business worked. Giovanni soon found better and more efficient ways do things and times improved for the company and for Giovanni.

The letters from home, pleading for him to return stopped after a few years. His family, still poor, but still proud, could not accept that Giovanni had become a 'manual worker'.

This was far from the truth: Giovanni had largely taken over the old man's role. The business had grown and with it, several new workers: they now printed the fliers, loaded the van and delivered them to customers. Giovanni was out being charming and his Italian looks got more and more business for the company. He'd began to think big and when the old man died, he saw his chance…

It was twenty years later: Giovanni, sitting in his office in a moderately successful printing company: glossy magazines, church newsletters, fliers – you name it, he printed it. A success in any terms. But the brooding had continued.

Despite what he told himself, "I have done alright for myself!" the memories kept coming back of his younger years and that surname.

He'd never be a statesman, never have glory, never be recognised in his native country as anything of greatness, but he had a wife who loved him, three kids he adored and he now owned the printing business.

When the bad memories came back, he'd sit in his office with a good bottle of wine (Italian of course), get drunk and brood, with the picture on the wall and a set of darts.

"Unify that!" he thought as the last dart thudded home, right between Garibaldi's eyes.

Sometimes Quite Cruel

When I was at school, sometime in the Cretaceous period, there was a girl in my class. Let's call her 'Ann'. Ann wanted to sing.

Unusually for my school, she was motivated to do something about it. With regular appearances at the front of the class, she would regale us with songs from musicals and the current pop charts. I used to sit there, embarrassed for her at the reception she got. It was usually total derision and utter contempt.

It was the sort of school that if you showed skills or talents, that would invite trouble. For girls it was derision and contempt, for clever boys, it invited aggression and violence. If you were wise, you kept your head down.

I accept that it was the spirit of the times. Most schools in my home town were useless and there was little innovation in how to encourage kids to learn. The teaching role was more than likely inspired by books on herding baboons than from any desire to impart knowledge. In any shape or form.

But up stood Ann and sang her little heart out. I know now that she was quite pretty, but at that age I didn't know my gluteus maximus from my radioulnar junction. There was something going on about her that I found fascinating and a bit disquieting, but I hadn't quite discovered why at that point.

Her favourite song was 'Wonderful Dream':

"You and I, we had a dream to fly
Wonderful dream, beautiful dream, don't let it die..."

Naturally I thought this a lot of tosh. I preferred Slade and later punk. This sentimental slop was far too syrupy for me. These days I realise it's perfect for teenage girls and useful for older teenage boys who want to get into their knickers.

Of course, I had no idea about that either! Ann did manage to get work on stage in her teens and did well for herself. The school did nothing for her, so presumably it was her talent and her parents' support who got her to that stage in her life.

I left school, got on with life as did she. About fifteen years later I heard a familiar voice at the railways station. "The train at platform five, is the..."

It was 'performed' almost like you'd imagine. Someone sitting in a small office telling people train times holding their nose to get that nasally impersonal sound beloved of station announcers. It sounded rather depressing and there was little spark of romance, love or knickers in it.

I caught my train and thought little more of it. Then a few years later, the train stations introduced computerised announcements. Now you have a machine with a synthetic voice telling you about train times, delays and security alerts.

So it would seem that poor Ann was denied the chance to sing, perform or even announce trains in a nasally disinterested fashion.

I think life is sometimes quite cruel.

Carry on Grandad

"Ooh Mr Rogers, I've lost control of me melons again!"

Grandad chortled, leering at the pretty young woman on the television screen who was chasing the fruit that rolled down the supermarket aisle.

"What I wouldn't give to get control of her melons," he roared at the top of his voice.

George sighed to himself. "Same stuff every day. Same old 'Carry On'. Same old sex-mad Grandad."

George's Grandad had dementia. He was forgetful, sometimes aggressive and couldn't be trusted to live on his own. Some people with dementia become unable to control their emotions.

"But Grandad has to turn into a deaf, randy old sod," thought George.

Grandad made life hell for any female visitor. It didn't matter to him if it was the care worker, the social worker, his daughter or his granddaughter. He was over familiar, invaded their personal space and made fruity suggestions. Very loudly and vigorously. Fortunately he'd done nothing else. Not yet, anyway.

It was George, his only Grandson who took on the burden. He called in once a day to make sure the old man was up, had breakfast and was seated in front of the television.

"Oh it's you. The ugly one," shouted the old man as George let himself in. "Why couldn't you be blonde and female with big…"

"I've got the latest 'Carry On' film for you, Grandad," interrupted the younger man.

The old man immediately stopped and a beautiful smile crossed his face.

"I hope it's got lots of pretty girls in it?" he asked hopefully. "They must have big…"

"Yes! All there for you, Grandad. Don't worry."

"Well don't bugger about, get it on. I wish I had someone I could 'Get it on' with, know what I mean?"

George sighed and ignored him.

The film started in the DVD player. It was clearly not an original 'Carry On' film and it bore the marks of poor editing and sound quality.

Grandad was entranced and for the next two hours there was silence, as he watched George's edited version of a 'Carry On' film. It was clips and vignettes from any and every film from the series George could find, edited into a format Grandad liked. Which meant buxom young woman and lots of cleavage.

George had seven of these films made up. It was enough so that by the time Grandad had watched the last one, he'd forgotten he'd ever watched the first. Round and round, the same homemade films, every day of the week.

"Why Miss Booby, I must insist that your melons remain in my care. You clearly can't keep your hands on them," muttered George to himself. He found himself joining in the dialogue which he now knew by heart.

George was in hell.

Uncle Pádraig

Pádraig was a bachelor farmer. He was a serious and quiet man who became bolder when he'd had a few drinks. Seamus would then argue with everyone to find out what they knew. He would never ask a straight question, preferring to argue and take against someone else's ideas to find out what they knew.

Pádraig didn't care much for his appearance. He had wild hair sprouting from his head, out his nose and from his ears. He looked nothing like the rest of the family. The rest of them privately called him 'the Fir Bolg'.

In the morning, Pádraig always looked a sight; unshaven, with mad hair and braces hanging down. He'd lift the cover of the range, snort and then spit into the fire.

I thought this was disgusting...

I can never remember him bathing, but he never smelt. He spent his days outside in the fresh air. Occasionally he reeked of pipe tobacco, which he broke up to make a cheap roll-up.

On Sunday mornings there would be a miraculous transformation. There would be the sounds of spluttering and splashing from the kitchen sink and suddenly he'd appear, shaved, hair tamed and wearing a smart grey suit. We'd all trawl off to Mass, but Seamus would stay outside, smoking with his cronies.

Despite a lack of formal education, Pádraig had practical intelligence. He'd taught himself how to fix broken farm equipment, his car and any electrics around the house. He was always disappointed if he had to pay money for repairs. The bane of his life was a nine inch 1950's television which regularly broke down. He'd refuse to replace it with anything that didn't have valves.

He was fascinated with science and after a few glasses of port, would hold forth on the universe, most of it taken from his 1936 astronomy book. His favourite theory was about "the circular nature of the universe" and "how light would eventually return to its source".

Someone in his audience would always tease, "Ah, Pádraig, if you'd care to sit there for a few billion years, I'm sure you'll eventually see the back of your own head."

A Decision Day

I was unsure what to do. Tomorrow was decision day...

I'd known Rob since I was a small child. The constant presence who lived next door and in the same classes at school. Rob was ordinary, lovely, and supportive. He seemed to plod along and was sort of charming. "Sexy," I thought. "Not a chance."

I longed for excitement!

Now, Adam. He was a babe. A bit of alright. Six foot tall, pale blue eyes and in the football team. And Adam liked and flirted with me constantly.

Rob sat down next to me and scowled.

"He's a rat, love."

"Are you jealous, Rob?" I laughed.

His face reddened. "No! He's just out to charm and get his leg over."

"What if I want that, Rob?"

"Then you'd better get on with it!" and he stormed off.

Rob avoided me for weeks. I tried to talk to him but he was "always busy" or I got a grunt in reply. If he saw me in the distance, he'd walk in the other direction.

But Adam! Wow! He took me out, wined and dined and loved me. Charmed and seduced. But he became possessive and angry when I talked to anyone else and especially other men. Rob kept his distance.

We went on like this throughout the rest of university life. I worked hard, but Adam just seemed to coast. When we got our results, he was furious. I got a 2:1 and he failed.

His response was with his fists.

The next day he was all apologies, begging forgiveness. Flowers in his hand. But I now knew what he was. I needed to get away.

I thought of Rob. Would he help? I phoned his parents and got his address.

He answered the door. "What the hell did he do to you?" he said as he let me in.

"How do you know it was Adam?" I asked.

"I know enough about people like Adam."

"Rob, I need somewhere to stay. I can't go back. I'm frightened he'll do it again."

Rob looked embarrassed. "You can't stay here. I'm sorry. You'll have to ask your Mum and Dad."

I looked at him despairingly. "You've always helped me before, Rob. Why can't you now, when I really need help?"

"It's not that I don't want to help, but it's... well, it's Josie."

"Who's Josie?"

"My girlfriend. She moved in six months ago. We're engaged."

It was then I saw the photos on the wall. Rob and a girl. Ordinary. Plain. Not 'sexy'. But it was the way they smiled at each other...

"Oh!" I said. "I'd better go..."

"I'm so sorry," said Rob. "I do hope you get yourself sorted out. Stay away from Adam, won't you?"

We said our goodbyes.

I never saw Rob ever again.

Staying Alive

Jean sighed. Everyone was up dancing and chatting. It was Yvonne's twenty-first, but Jean was stuck with her Dad. Everyone else was enjoying themselves, but the two of them sat in silence, Jean watching and Dad lost in thought.

"If he's even here at all," she thought to herself.

She watched the dancers, especially the younger men and felt jealous. Since her divorce there had been no-one. And she couldn't remember the last time she'd had sex. "Eighteen months?" she thought.

She longed to be out there, dancing with the young guys. Just a bit of harmless flirting. That would do. Just to be noticed by someone young and virile. But not when she had to babysit Dad.

Her divorce was mercifully trouble-free. Derek had taken little interest in her for several years and their love life gradually wound down like a broken clockwork toy. She smiled to herself. A toy boy would be better.

She looked over at her Dad again. Ninety-five years old. Shrunken, quiet and uncooperative. He'd been just like that all day. Wherever she wanted him to sit, he'd want to sit elsewhere. Whenever she ordered food for him, he wanted something else. All passive aggressive and difficult. It was easier to agree with him than have to shout to make herself understood.

It was a far cry from the Dad of her childhood and early twenties. Always laughing, always active, the dancing classes with her Mum. She was embarrassed then. People in their fifties shouldn't learn to disco dance! But even then she could see the joy it gave them. She wished Dad and her late Mum could share that joy now.

He'd always been a restless spirit but good-humoured. Job to job to job, but always with a good reference and the affection of everyone he worked with. He charmed and was kind and he treated everyone the same.

Now that was all gone. Silently shuffling around on his walking frame. The life had gone out of him since her Mum had died.

Jean sighed and went back to watching the dancers. And especially the fit young men.
The DJ's voice boomed out around the dance-floor. "And now let's have some 'Saturday Night Fever'. There was a big cheer from the crowd as the sound of 'Stayin' Alive' came over the speakers.

She smiled at the happy gyrating crowd. She didn't notice Dad until he was up and moving with his zimmer.

"Dad! Dad! Where are you going?"

"I'm going to dance," he said.

"You can't dance, you'll fall!"

"I'm going to dance," he said, determination in his voice. She knew it was futile to argue when he used that tone.

Dad shuffled over to the dancing crowd who parted to let him in, Jean following. He stood for a moment, taking the crowd in. And then he started to move...

The years fell off him as he danced and wobbled and smiled his way through 'Stayin' Alive'. The crowd roared their approval as he worked his way through the routine, and the more he danced, the more energised and daring he became.

When the song ended, his energy went too. Jean caught him as he stumbled and got him back on the zimmer. Everyone was clapping and cheering Dad as he slowly made his way back to his seat.

"You were fabulous, Dad! You've still got all the moves!"

The old man smiled. "Not dead yet, Jean. You know how much your Mum and I loved..." and then he stopped. "Go and have a dance. Meet a nice young man. Don't waste your life with a silly old bugger like me! No...! Go on..."

She got onto the dance floor, trying to position herself to see her Dad, but he had gone back into himself again. Quiet and unmoving. She found herself dancing with one of her cousin's friends. "What was his name? Richard? Rich!"

Rich was probably ten years younger than her, but he was clearly enjoying dancing with her. She basked in his attention.

"He's gorgeous!" she thought. "What can he see in me?"

They spent the night dancing and she hoped for more. "Would you like to go somewhere else, Rich?"

"I'd love to, Jean, but I'm driving down to Southampton tomorrow morning. Give me your number. Could we go out next Friday?"

Of course he never called. But she started dance classes two weeks later and met a nice guy from

Leicester. They both loved disco and later, each other.

Potential, Interrupted

Josh woke to the stabbing pain in his head and the urge to be sick.

"Another hangover," he thought. "How many this week?"

It was becoming a bad habit, but it was also the only thing that relaxed him and made him switch off. Otherwise it was thinking, thinking, thinking, far into the night and the thoughts were seldom happy.

He often disliked himself, but at the same time wondered if anyone else would feel any different in the same situation. Home, parents, school, work. A series of slow bubbling unhappiness.

Josh thought back to his early days. His parents. "So bloody holy and so bloody holier than thou..."

They were very, very religious. Two visits to their church on a Sunday and prayers before every meals. And again at night. Josh had a diet rich in piety, but poor in mercy.

It was almost as if his parents had never been children themselves. They seemed forever old. Everything revolved around Bible reading, or Bible study, or Bible reflection. They appeared to hate and fear the world around them. No television, radio or newspapers were allowed in the house.

Josh was their ongoing disappointment. The boy showed little interest in Bible reading and he frequently misbehaved. The church minister was the focus of intense conversations about Josh and 'unclean spirits'.

Despite the minster's assurances ("All young boys can be a little wild at times"), Josh's parents were convinced he was 'bad'. Josh was prayed over, doused in holy water and occasionally beaten for his 'sins'.

Nothing worked. Josh thrived at school in the arts and science, but showed little interest in the evangelism his parents demanded. As he got into his teens, his behaviour at home got worse and it spilled over into school and his friendships.

"I forbid you to associate with those sinner boys!" shouted his father. Josh, nonetheless, went out and kicked a football around with his mates. Their parents seemed a lot more laid back and all of them did their best to show some affection to him.

"That poor kid. His mother and father are fanatics!"

It got worse as Josh hit puberty. His mother's ongoing lectures about "the sins of the flesh" just made him curious and he had started to notice that girls were interesting. By sixteen he had a secret, but steady girlfriend and he spent as much time as he could with her. The beautiful Anna...

The beautiful Anna! He adored her, he worshipped her (and got a perverse sense of pleasure from thinking that) and he wanted to give her everything he had. But he had nothing.

Other boys had pocket money, part-time jobs and the latest fashions. Poor drab Josh, dressed in hand-me-downs that looked like something out of the 1950s, could not compete. He wasn't allowed to get a job because it interfered with his parents' endless prayer routines.

"Mammon cannot compete with the word of God, you ungrateful boy!"

"I really like you, Josh," Anna said, "But I'm fed up with holding hands at the bus stop or sitting on park benches. I want to live a little!"

Anna dumped him and started going out with Francis: he was flash, well dressed, had a job in the evening, bought cinema tickets and even had enough money to take Anna to 'Pizza Hut'.

By seventeen, Josh was in full revolt. He'd been spotted by his father washing cars at a local garage, who then launched into a preaching session on 'the wickedness and the ungratefulness of children' and 'his association with vagabonds and sinners'.

"Is that really your Dad, mate?" asked Brian, one of his workmates.

"Yeah, he is."

"No offence, Josh, but is he a loony?"

"I think so. Both him and my mother. It's just 'Bible this, Bible that...' all day and all night. I wish I could get away."

"Then why don't you?"

Josh's father then attempted to drag him away from his workmates. So Josh hit him in the scuffle. There was a fifteen minute monologue from his father, while he held his eye, "Cutting you off like the disease you are! You are no longer my son!"

And then he stormed off.

As Josh calmed down, he realised the mess he was in. "What am I going to do? Where am I going to go?"

"Tell you what, come stay with me, mate," said Brian, one of Josh's workmates.

"But won't you have to ask your parents?"

Brian laughed. "Parents? I left home a year ago. We're in a squat. We don't mind new faces. Come on..."

Josh was welcomed by nearly everyone at the squat. They fed him and treated him like he was a human being.

"You'll have to bring some money in though, Josh."

"How?"

"Washing cars won't do it. Have you ever had a smoke?"

"No, my parents didn't approve of cigarettes."

Brain laughed. "Yeah. 'Cigarettes'. Well let's try a cigarette or two shall we?"

That was Josh's first experience of being high, but not his last. Over the next few weeks Brian introduced him to beer, marijuana, amphetamines and eventually to sex.

"Watch out for Tommy. He likes you. If you've got a girl he'll leave you alone."

Josh washed cars in the day and sold drugs at night. He made a decent amount of money out of it, but most of it was taken off him by Brian and the others at the squat. "Got to pay your fair share, mate!"

Over time, Josh got lost in drink, dope and sex and it made him happy for a while. He forgot about his mother and father and just lived for the now. But he noticed how the others had begun to sneer at him and Jasmine, who he slept with became more reluctant.

"Every time I go near her, she rolls her eyes. Like she's doing me a big favour. I've got to get out of here."

He mentioned this to Brian who encouraged more spliffs, more drinking and there was more enthusiasm from Jasmine. At least for a while.

He started to hide some of the money he made at night. When they caught him, Tommy beat him up and they all kicked him out the door. He was penniless, roughed up and on the street. What was he going to do?

Echo and Gas Chamber

@NigelM1936: Hi there welcome to this weeks #WeCare where we show the world how we care about poor people and the #underworkingclass

JulieFluffycake: Hi guys we love #WeCare because we care about everyone! :-) Even the #underworkingclass

NigelM1936: Whose with us tonight showcasing the great work of #WeCare?

@UKActionFront: Hey! We love you @NigelM1936 @deniseopenaccess @jorgefranco look fwd to #WeCare wisdom this week. Love you guys lots! #WeCare

@deniseopenaccess: Hey whose here? I'm here! Remember that #work is a #goodthing and frees you from your cares #WeCare

@NigelM1936: #WeCare Hi Denise we're honoured to have you here – how did your rally go last week? You were so cool I know. I don't have to ask :-)

@deniseopenaccess: HI Nigel we had so much fun so many people all wanting to hear our message and our new slogan about work and freedom

@UKActionFront: #WeCare rocks! ;-)

@NigelM1936: RT @deniseopenaccess HI Nigel we had so much fun so many people all wanting to hear our message and our new slogan about work and freedom #WeCare

@NigelM1936: Don't forget the #hashtag #WeCare guys! :-P

@JulieFluffycake: Don't keep us hangin we love that work makes us freer to do what we want & what #WeCare needs

@deniseopenaccess: @UKActionFront rocks too! where would we be without your #WeCare support dude

@jorgefranco Hey I'm late! I hope #Leader @deniseopenaccess isn't mad at me! ;-) #WeCare

@deniseopenaccess: Hey Jorge we're honoured to have your contribution Ur awareness of how #WeCare #inspiration to all

@NigelM1936: Where's @Juntafan? We miss you dude! #WeCare not the same without you!

@deniseopenaccess: It would be cool to become @LeaderDenise waddya you guys think? ☺ @WeCare

@NigelM1936: Go for it #Leader we'll follow you wherever you wanna go to show #WeCare

@jorgefranco: you guys should know my new blog #workmakesUfree is up I value what all the #WeCare people think

@UKActionFront: RT @NigelM1936 Where's @Juntafan? We miss you dude! #WeCare not the same without you!

@bulldogdave1966 Hi I'm new what do you do here? #WeCare

@NigelM1936: welcome @bulldogdave1966 to #WeCare where we show the world how much #caring helps the world 2 find a #newworldorder

@UKActionFront: I wanna see that blog now @jorgefranco #WeCare we love you dude!

@bulldogdave1966: Sounds interesting so what do you do to get there? #WeCare

@NigelM1936: We've got three million #WeCare tweets this last year @bulldogdave1966

@jorgefranco: Thanks @UKActionFront really value your feedback we couldn't do this without you. Getting people into dignified labour situations is one of the #firstsolutions #WeCare wanna raise. Final ones later dude

;-)

@JulieFluffycake: #WeCare is A-MAZ-ING! :-)

@bulldogdave1966: So lots of slogans but not much action yet. That's OK but what will you do? #workmakesUfree sounds a bit sinister you know? #WeCare

@jorgefranco: We can do this with or without you @bulldogdave1966 we need +ve vibes not anyone dragging us back #WeCare

@UKActionFront: You're A-MAZ-ING too @JulieFluffycake! ;-) #WeCare #amazing

@deniseopenaccess: is now @LeaderDenise

@LeaderDenise: HI guys waddya think of the new nick? #WeCare #leader #care

@bulldogdave1966: I don't mean to cause trouble it's just some of your phrases could be offensive to some people #WeCare

@NigelM1936: love it babe @LeaderDenise is what you are we'll follow you to show #WeCare when no-one else doesn't

@UKActionFront: we don't like newbies tellin us what we should say @bulldogdave1966 maybe you should just listen learn @LeaderDenise knows & we know too #WeCare

@LeaderDenise #WeCare #UfollowIlead just go with the group @bulldogdave1966 & you'll see it's for your good & everyone so that #YouCare as much as #WeCare

@JulieFluffycake: I wanna follow @LeaderDenise @NigelM1936 @jorgefranco you tell me where and #WeCare together but tell me just say how

@NigelM1936: Next week we have a special guest @joegoebb whose gonna tell us about what to do with #jobless. We need solutions to help #underworkingpeople who won't #work #WeCare #firstsolutions #finalsolutions

@bulldogdave1966: you lot are weird you expect me to follow you blindly & agree to some weird agenda #WeCare This chat is hot air just a gas chamber I'm off! :-(

@LeaderDenise: #finalsolutions would be so cool no more being gentle when people have real needs that #WeCare WE know better and they don't dontcha think?

@jorgefranco: @joegoebb is so inspiring! I love his website #WeCare

@UKActionFront: It's sad when #people or # underworkingpeople don't know what's good for them. We'll have to make 'em! ☺ #WeCare will show them the way! :-)

@UKActionFront: don't come back @bulldogdave1966 if you can't fit in theres some #solution #finalsolution for you too if you won't do as we nicely suggested #WeCare #4yourgood

@NigelM1936: I love @joegoebb too! #WeCare

@jorgefranco: Let's #empower # underworkingpeople help them get what they #want #need the #WeCare way

@LeaderDenise: Maybe we should just call them #underpeople? #WeCare Easy to remember #hashtag! ☺

@UKActionFront: yeah lets show them what they need & inspire them the #WeCare way! And sort out the one's that can't or won't?

@JulieFluffycake: it's so true! @LeaderDenise can show us all that #WeCare and if nasty people like @bulldogdave1966 can't see they'll have to be made too as well! Is he #underpeople too? :-(

@NigelM1936: chill @JulieFluffycake I blocked @bulldogdave1966 but I have him on my list when our @WeCare #solutions #finalsolutions show that #workmakesUfree

@JulieFluffycake: I love @joegoebb too! #WeCare

@jorgefranco: I'm so #excited we've got @joegoebb here on #WeCare next week! ☺☺☺

@NigelM1936: #underpeople is SO cool! #WeCare

@jorgefranco: So wise @JulieFluffycake we're privileged to have you here every week at #WeCare

@JulieFluffycake: RT @NigelM1936 #underpeople is SO cool! #WeCare

@JulieFluffycake: #underpeople is the #newblack haha! :-) #WeCare

@jorgefranco: you guys are so much fun! We have momentum now & we'll show the world a new way to a #WeCare world where #underpeople are taken care of

@UKActionFront: I'm #loyal we're #onetweeters #onehashtag #oneleader #WeCare

@NigelM1936: @LeaderDenise #leadercommand We're with you! #WeCare and one day the world will #care too

@LeaderDenise: y'know you guys give me so much support and I love being your #Leader I wanna be your #WeCare #Leader! We just need some #breathingspace to show #WeCare

@jorgefranco: Be our @Leader @LeaderDenise #WeCare

@UKActionFront: RT @jorgefranco Be our @Leader @LeaderDenise #WeCare

@JulieFluffycake: RT @jorgefranco Be our @Leader @LeaderDenise #WeCare

@LeaderDenise I love you guys! I'm gonna be your @Leader it's time. History is on our side! We will show the whole world how much #WeCare I'm gonna change my nick again! :-P

@LeaderDenise is now @Leader

@NigelM1936: Be our #WeCare @Leader we raise our hand to you!

@UKActionFront: Be our #WeCare @Leader we raise our hand to you!

@jorgefranco: Be our #WeCare @Leader we raise our hand to you!

@jorgefranco: #onetweeters #onehashtag #oneleader – love it @UKActionFront! #WeCare so much #care here #WeCare together

@Leader It's time. #worlddoesntcare but #WeCare!

@Leader: It won't change and won't #care but #WeCare!

@Leader: #WeCare over all!

@Leader #WeCare and we'll sort out the #underpeople who won't embrace #workmakesUfree

@NigelM1936: Such powerful tweets @Leader Everyone can see that #youcare and #WeCare too! :-)

@Leader: It's time to make the world #Care & become part of #WeCare Who is with me?

@JulieFluffycake: If these #underpeople won't take risks we'll do it for them @Leader knows whats best for them #worksmakesUfree we'll #free them

@UKActionFront: I'm with you @Leader #WeCare rules!

@jorgefranco: we're with you @Leader #WeCare rules!

@UKActionFront: I'm always with you @Leader #WeCare rules!

@JulieFluffycake: I'm loyal to you @Leader #WeCare rules!

@JuntaFan: Hey guys sorry I'm late! I love our @Leader! #WeCare #ILoveOurLeader #workmakesUfree

@JulieFluffycake: welcome @JuntaFan we love you I'm proud to know you #WeCare

@JulieFluffycake: we missed you @JuntaFan #WeCare

@Leader: Hey @JuntaFan so joyous to have you here and your support #WeCare

@JuntaFan: Love you guys too! :-) #WeCare It's great to meet and rally to the #WeCare cause!

@JuntaFan: So much #wisdom here! :-) #WeCare

@JulieFluffycake: RT @JuntaFan So much #wisdom here! :-) #WeCare

@NigelM1936: RT @JuntaFan So much #wisdom here! :-) #WeCare

@jorgefranco: RT @JuntaFan So much #wisdom here! :-) #WeCare

@Leader: RT @JuntaFan So much #wisdom here! :-) #WeCare

@UKActionFront: we're all learning from you @JuntaFan So much #WeCare #wisdom every week!

@JuntaFan: You guys are so much fun! :-) #WeCare

@Leader: we couldn't do it without you @Juntafan We love you #WeCare

@jorgefranco: You inspire us @Juntafan We love you #WeCare

@JulieFluffycake: we love you @JuntaFan #WeCare

@NigelM1936: You bring so much to the movement @Juntafan #WeCare

@JuntaFan: Guys I'm blushing :-) I wanna follow the #WeCare @Leader

@UKActionFront: You guys are #totally #cool #WeCare

@Leader: Any dissenters? :-(#WeCare

@UKActionFront: Not me #WeCare @Leader

@JulieFluffycake: Not me #WeCare @Leader

@jorgefranco: Never me #WeCare @Leader

@UKActionFront: we'll sort the dissenters ☹
#WeCare @Leader

@Leader: Didn't think so :-) #WeCare

@Leader: #WeCare And your loyalty will be
rewarded

@Leader: We're #onetweeters #onehashtag
#oneleader #WeCare

@UKActionFront: RT @Leader We're
#onetweeters #onehashtag #oneleader #WeCare

@NigelM1936: RT @Leader We're #onetweeters
#onehashtag #oneleader #WeCare

@jorgefranco : RT @Leader We're #onetweeters #onehashtag #oneleader #WeCare

@JuntaFan: RT @Leader We're #onetweeters #onehashtag #oneleader #WeCare

@Leader #WeCare rocks! ☺☺☺

The Laff Brothers – a true story

Francis and Frederick Laughton were born in Chorley, Lancashire. The twins were precocious from an early age. Franny was quiet, thoughtful and clever with words and jokes, while Freddie was always messing about, playing practical jokes and talking in silly voices. Freddie was a natural mimic.

At school they became known at the 'Laffton Brothers' and were the source of jokes and fun throughout the school, but they both left education with no qualifications and were soon working at the local steel mill.

Francis and Freddie hated the dangerous work and continued to cause mayhem whenever they could. They were spotted in the town by the impresario, Richard Bach, who got them to sit down and put together some ideas for an act, called 'The Laff Brothers'.

It worked well. Franny was full of ideas and Freddie fed off his brother's imagination with physical pranks and voices. They were soon entertaining people in pubs and clubs around the area and they made a reasonable living out of it. When the mill owners heard about their night-time work, they were immediately sacked.

Then came years on the road, working around the northern club circuit, but becoming well known in the Midlands and later in the south. Their mixture of word play, surreal and physical comedy with mimicry made them very popular. Bach, now their manager, received an offer for them to have a thirty minute radio show at the BBC.

The Laff Brothers were a raging success and soon had a regular slot on 'The Light Program'. They still continued to tour heavily and record for the BBC. But the cracks had started to show...

Franny resented Freddie for his outgoing personality and the attention it got. "That bloody show-off. It's my writing that makes it happen and he gets the all credit," he thought.

Freddie in turn was jealous of Franny for the clever lines and wordplay that he spoke, but seldom understood. "If he'd only do it my way, we'd do a lot better. Less talking blather and more being funny..."

They began to fall our regularly as one tried to outdo the other. Franny's jokes got cleverer and more obscure and Freddie's antics went beyond humour into farce. They simply stopped being funny.

By the time their contract at the BBC had ended, they were no longer talking. 'That knobhead with his over-clever ideas' had no time for 'silly dickhead with his pratfalls'. Richard Bach ended up being a constant intermediary between the two brothers as the two would never speak outside of their act. They eventually split after a furious argument that nearly came to blows.

Their solo careers were a disaster. 'Francis Laughton' had some success as a stand-up comedian, but his humour was too subtle and cerebral for a mainstream audience. His fame quickly faded and in the end, no-one wanted to see him or read his scripts.

Freddie was even worse off. His solo career ended as soon as it began. The review were harsh: 'Childish voices and falling over'. 'My ten year old would be embarrassed to watch such antics'. 'We suggest Freddie Laff get a decent scriptwriter'.

The last comment was the most hurtful.

Both brothers struggled to get work. Francis found work in a small theatre company working around northern England, while Freddie became a landlord in a Chorley pub. Freddie's open and friendly manner got lots of customers, but he began to drink heavily.

The brothers had not seen each other for twenty years when his theatre company went for a quick drink at a local pub after a performance. Francis was bored to death with his job, but he needed the money and the people were easy to work with.

Jonno, the company manager got the drinks in. When he came back he looked puzzled.

"Francis, there's a bloke behind the bar who's the spitting image of you. Looks a bit worse for wear, though. Face like a beetroot. Bit fond of his drink it looks like. Half-cut already."

Francis was intrigued. "I'll have a look. Back in a minute."

He was shocked. It was Freddie. But he looked terrible and was as drunk as a sack.

"Freddie! Freddie" he called out. "It's me, Franny!"

Freddie looked up, swaying as he blurrily looked over the bar.

"Bloody hell, it's you! Still writing smart-arse jokes nobody gets?"

"Not really, Freddie. I work for a theatre company."

"How very la-di-da of you."

"Don't be like that, Freddie."

"'Don't be like that' mimicked Freddie. "If it wasn't for you, I'd still be famous. Loads of money, loads of booze and loads of girls. We had it made and you buggered it up for us!"

"Me? You had no ideas and all you did in the end was talk in daft voices no-one found funny and endless falling or tripping over your own feet. No-one laughed at that either, but you kept on with it and no-one could tell you otherwise."

"Well if you don't like it, my dear clever clogs brother, why are you in my lovely pub?"

"Purely by accident. I can assure you it won't happen again!"

Francis stormed over to the table and spoke to the actors waiting. "I'll be back at the B&B."

They were astonished at him. The normally quiet and unflappable Francis was purple with rage.

His brother shouted after him. "Don't come back. Go and ruin somebody else's life..." before he went over a crate and down with a crash.

The regulars laughed. Freddie still liked to mess about and his 'trips' were a regular feature for his customers. When he didn't reappear, a few of them came behind the bar and found him still on the floor. Freddie's face was pale as bright red blood ran from the cut on his forehead.

There was a flurry of interest from the press when the news was announced. Francis wanted to go to the funeral, but he turned away when he saw the mass of reporters.

For months he was pestered by journalists to tell the story of 'poor Freddie'. The money would have come in handy, but he always said 'No'.

Caninute

Scarborough.

Sun. Blue skies. Castle. Sweep of the bay.
Trawlers in the distance. An oil tanker or two.
Tatty pound shops. The smell of candy floss and
fish and chips. Seaside organ music. Not too
many people.

Perfect!

But there's a little dog trying to stop the tide
coming in...

Every wave was greeted by a snarl as the Jack
Russell chased it to the shore. Then back out to
sea for the next.

I can tell when a dog is having fun. This one
wasn't. Something about the moving water

deeply offended him and he was determined to make it stop.

After a few minutes a small crowd formed, laughing at the dog's antics as running sideways he yapped at every ocean movement. He ignored his master's whistles and calls as he jumped further out to tackle the next swell.

A sudden surge swamped him completely and he disappeared under ice cold water, only to suddenly reappear, sodden and surprised. With a 'yelp' he struggled to the shoreline, gave himself a shake and then went straight back into the current.

His owner, a large sunburnt man in his sixties, had had enough. "Jack, you little bugger! Come on!"

'Jack' continued to try to halt the tide, batting at each wave with his right paw. He was eventually pulled away from his sea-battle, first by collar and then by leash.

His red-faced owner stomped off into the distance, dragging the little dog behind him, who still made darting runs at the water.

Monkey Tea Free Zone

Mick sometimes wondered about his Mum. Specifically about her sanity. She'd got upset again. About tea.

It had gone on as long as he could remember. As a child, his Mum flatly refused to buy 'PG Tips'. Loose tea or bags, PG Tips was right out.

"Dat monkey tea! I'm not havin' dat monkey tea in my house!"

Even as a child, Mick tried to explain. "But just because it's advertised using chimpanzees, it doesn't mean they make it, Mum?"

"I don't care. Just look at them. Dirty! A hideous caricature of humanity. Playing the piano. Roller skating. What next for heaven's sake?"

It was a lost cause. Any other brand was allowed, but the thought of chimps having anything to do with Mum's favourite brew generated an hysterical reaction. Eventually, when Mick was in his twenties, the truth came out.

"Do you remember when I had to go to Wales for your cousin's wedding?"

"Yes, I do. I wish I could have come with you. I got stuck with Dad for a week. Half raw boiled potatoes and he thought sausages should be boiled too. And don't get me started on him adding half a loaf of breadcrumbs to a tin of salmon 'to make it go further'."

"Well you couldn't come with me. It was a sensitive matter. You were too young."

"What was it about, then?"

"You're still too young."

"Mum, I'm twenty-five!"

"Still too young."

"How old will I have to be?" Mick asked.

Mum gave one of her rare impish grins. "A bit younger than God. Then I'll tell..."

Mick couldn't help but smile back.

"No, it was your idiot father taking you to the zoo."

"Oh? What was wrong with that?"

"It was that damned monkey who grabbed you and your brother, Stephen."

Mick suddenly remembered. He was six years old and a chimpanzee had grabbed him and his brother as the keeper took the animal 'off for his nap'.

He recalled its strength, as it grasped him by his anorak and Stephen by the belt. Nothing was going to make the chimpanzee let go, but there was no sense of threat. "It just wanted some company," Mick thought.

It all ended peacefully. The monkey let go when he got to his quarters. The other chimps hooted in greeting and the crisis was over. It was exciting for a six year old, but quickly forgotten.

"When your father told me I nearly died! I was all set to come home to make sure you were both unhurt. The big eejit! How he could let you get into danger like that?"

"But no-one was hurt, Mum. I can barely remember it."

"I swore there'd be no more monkey business in this family!"

Mick started to laugh. There had been far more 'monkey business' in the family home than either Mum or Dad had ever been aware of.

"What are you laughing at?" she asked.

"Nothing. I just think it's funny you've refused to buy a brand of tea because of an over-friendly young chimpanzee twenty years ago."

"Over-friendly? It could have eaten you alive!"

Mick sighed, "I doubt that. So now you've told me, can I buy you some PG Tips?"

"No! I don't care what anyone thinks. I'll never allow monkey tea in this house. Not as long as I'm alive!"

Mick shrugged. He'd learnt his lesson. "Fair enough. I'll have a coffee, then."

Pork

"'ello mate you don't mind me sitting here do you?"

"Well actually…"

"No worries mate, I'm sure I can make room for anyone else who might turn up."

"Sorry I was waiting…"

"…pork!"

"I beg your pardon?"

"I bet you don't feed your dog pork, do you, mate?"

"I'm sorry, do I know you?"

"No, mate, but I can tell by looking at you that you would never feed your dog pork."

"I'm so sorry, you must be confusing me with someone else. I don't have a dog."

"You don't? Shame. But if you did, would you feed your dog pork?"

"I have no idea, I don't own a dog. I've never owned a dog."

"Fair enough, but you look like a bloke who should own a dog. I bet you'd never feed you dog pork if you owned one."

"I'm allergic to dog's, I'm afraid, it's their fur."

"I bet if you stopped feeding your dog pork, you'd be fine, mate."

"I'm sorry I have no idea…"

"…it's a well-known fact, mate, that lots of dog allergies is caused by owners feeding their dog pork."

"I couldn't possibly…"

"…see, I've never fed my dog pork."

"That's nice, but…"

"It stands to reason that I've got no allergies because I've never fed my dog pork. It's scienttypically proved. Quid pro status quo!"

"Actually it's 'Quid pro…'"

"…I've never fed my Milly pork. Never. EVER!"

"Milly? Who is…?"

"…no feeding my dog pork!"

"Oh I see, I thought…"

"…have you ever owned a Jack Russell, mate?"

"No, as I said…"

"…I bet you've never fed it pork have you mate."

"No, I've never…"

"…fed it pork, I know where your coming from, mate! I could see when my eyes met yours across a crowded room, that we were soul mates…"

"I think you might be confusing…"

"I saw you 'ere and thought immediately we was two peas in a 'none feeding your dog pork' pod."

"I keep telling you I've never owned a dog!"

"What, never?"

"Never, ever!"

"Are you sure?"

"Yes!"

"Ever associated with a dog?"

"No..."

"Ever associated with a dog and accidentally fed it pork?"

"No, why don't you listen..."

"Not even not feeding your mate's dog pork accidentally?"

"Yes, quite sure! Especially feeding it…"

"…no Golden Retriever?"

"No!"

"Labrador?"

"No!"

"You shouldn't feed them pork either, mate…"

"I haven't got any dog! I don't like dogs!"

"Shitzu?"

"I beg your pardon?"

"Just a joke mate, but you should never, ever, feed your Shitzu pork!"

"I don't know anything about dogs!"

"But at least you know now you shouldn't feed your dog pork, mate".

"I don't care about dogs!"

"But you'd care enough not to feed your dog pork, mate, wouldn't you?"

"Oh for the love of God…"

"Ah, there's another connection! A religious man, I knew it! Just like St Francis of Assisi, he liked God and he liked dogs. We were meant to be together, mate."

"Yes, St Francis is well known for his kindness to animals. What's that got...?"

"I bet he never fed his dog pork."

"How on earth do you know that?"

"It stands to reason, mate. He loved animals and dogs especially, I can tell you. And if he loved dogs he would never feed his dog pork."

"You know that definitively?"

"It's obvious, mate. Old St Francis loved God and dogs but hated the Devil and pork, which amounts to the same thing, strictly between you and me, mate!"

"Cynthia! Cynthia! Over here!"

"Hello darling, I'm so sorry I'm late!"

"That's fine darling, let's go, we have an urgent appointment somewhere else!"

"Is that your girlfriend, mate?"

"This is Cynthia, yes!"

"'ello darlin'! I bet you wouldn't feed your dog pork?"

"Why is that?"

"Err... well... you just don't!"

"But I want to know why I shouldn't feed my dog pork. There must be a reason?"

"...sorry mate, sorry darlin', must be off, no dawdling for a busy 'don't feed his dog pork' sort of bloke like me. See you later..."

A Degree of Awareness

I queued up with all the others in my class, waiting to go on stage. I was nervous, as usual. I hated fuss and public appearances and standing up in front of others.

Paddy Amity was up first, with a cheery grin on his face, chatting away to everyone, ten to the dozen as usual, a complete contrast to me, with my silence and brooding.

It was all coming to an end.

I thought I'd never see Paddy, Chris, Louise, Francis or any of my classmates and other friends again. We'd all scatter to our home towns or off to London, Manchester or wherever the jobs were. I'd especially miss Paddy and Louise. My eyes smarted with tears.

"Mark, you big eejit, cheer up!" laughed Paddy.

I smiled back at him. "Bugger off, you'd be laughing at your own funeral."

"I would. And what's wrong with that, you miserable northern fecker?"

"It's the end, mate."

"No, it's the beginning..." Paddy replied.

"Of what?"

"Of our lives. We're all going off and start doing other things. What's wrong with that?"

"I'll miss you all, that's what."

"And I'll miss you. But not your sulking. Put a smile on that face and at least pretend to enjoy the day."

I laughed back. "Just for you, darling!"

"Come on, we've got to be given a blank piece of paper by some British aristocrat we've never heard of..."

There she stood: Lady Truscott-Fowley, patron of the college and human rights campaigner. I'd never heard of her, then. Stern and commanding. A right battle-axe. She looked like she'd rather be leading troops into battle than giving out degree certificates.

Paddy walked out onto the stage.

"Patrick Amity, Bachelor with Honours Electronic Engineering, with a First."

He crossed the stage so confidently, the little git. All swagger and charm. There was a roar from his family, out in the audience. He turned to the crowd and took his mortar board hat off with a florid bow. Paddy the showman as ever!

The crowd laughed at him and he smiled too as he took the parchment from Lady Truscott-Fowley's hand. Even she smiled back, charmed by his antics and his cheek.

Then it was the others from my class. Louise looked beautiful and elegant in a way I hadn't noticed before. And clever too! A First! She was sure footed and confident, but with a hint of a blush. She took the parchment, smiled and left the stage. My eyes followed her. My friend and classmate is beautiful. Luminous and gorgeous.

I shook my head to clear these thoughts. "She's my pal!" I thought. "A good friend. That's all."

Others were called forward and suddenly it was me. "Mark Smith, Bachelor with Honours Electronic Engineering, with a 2:1."

I tried to walk slowly but I couldn't think straight.

"Don't trip up, don't trip up, don't trip up," I mumbled to myself.

I shook the Lady's hand and promptly dropped the certificate. Everyone laughed and I blushed bright red. I quickly picked it up and spotted one of my lecturers, Professor Susan Chambers, at the back. One of the few favourites from my studies. I nodded and give her a wink. She smiled back. Then I scurried off the stage.

I remember nothing else. I was so relieved to be out of the spotlight. My friends were together chatting excitedly and they all turned to greet me.

"There, that wasn't so bad, was it Mark?" asked Louise, as she tucked her arm in mine. Her closeness and perfume made me feel dizzy.

"I suppose not. Thank God it's over, though!"

Their families came over to join us, but as usual I had no-one of my own. My Dad took no interest in me or my learning and Mum always followed his lead. There would be no fussing and pride about my achievements. Ever.

I moved away and watched them all. Paddy with his tribe, clustered loudly around him, hugging and kissing and congratulating him over and over. I felt a flash of jealousy, but I was pleased for him. Clever and confident, we hit it off from day one. I'd miss him very much, but someone else much more...

I looked over at Louise standing with what must be her Mum and Dad. They were quiet, but bursting with pride for their daughter. Just a kiss and a brief hug, but they couldn't keep their eyes off her, like she was the radiant sun shining in the sky. I shook my head again. "Where is all this coming from?"

Everywhere I looked, I saw families and friends together. And then there was me.

"Time to go," I thought to myself.

I was walking away when a male voice shouted my name.

"Mark! Mark! Just a minute."

I turned. It was Louise's Dad?

"Hello, Mark. I'm Louise's father, Nick. Can I have a quick word?"

I forced a smile. "Of course, Mr Jones. How can I help?"

"Call me Nick, Mark. Let's go over here out the way."

He stops, as if he's thinking what to say.

"Louise tells me your parents didn't come to see you graduate?"

"No. It's my Dad. 'Education is a load of bunkum' is all he ever had to say. I'm just as happy he's not here to be honest. He'd only spoil it for me and everyone else."

"That's a shame. Would you like to join us?" Nick asked.

I shook my head. "No, honestly, I wouldn't want to intrude. Have a lovely day with Louise. You must be so proud of her."

"I am. And her mother too. Look, Mark, I don't know how to say this properly. Do you like my daughter?"

I was taken aback. "Louise? I love her to bits. She's a great pal and I wish her the best of everything in her future."

Nick looked puzzled for a moment. "Do you have any idea how Louise feels about you?"

"Feels about me? What do you mean?"

Nick laughed. "You really don't, do you?"

"I have no idea..."

"Louise's phone calls to me and my wife are all about you. It's 'Mark this...' and 'Mark that...' and how much she likes you. But it's mostly about how you don't seem to like her back."

"Is this a joke, Nick?" I replied, a little annoyed.

"Of course not. We're talking about my daughter here. Her happiness means more to me than anything else in the world. Except for my wife, of course. You, young man, are the key to Louise's happiness, it seems. Clueless or not."

I looked over at Louise talking to her Mum. When she noticed me, she gave me a radiant smile and motioned at me to come over.

"See?" said Nick.

"I had no idea... she never said... what a dickhead I am!"

He grinned back at me. "Yes, you are, Mark. But not the first and not the last young man when it comes to understanding women. What are you going to do about it?"

"I should go over and talk to her?"

Nick slapped me on the back and smiled. "A good start! Let's get going then."

We dodged the crowds to walk over to Louise and her Mum.

Nick introduced us. "Janet, this is Mark. Mark, this is my wife, Janet."

Janet looked me up and down and smirked. "Oh, you're Mark? Well, I can see why Louise likes you."

Louise reddened. "Mum, you're embarrassing Mark. And me too."

"Only seeing what's right in front of me, darling," her Mum replied.

"Janet. We just need to have a chat with Louise's tutor before it's too late."

Mum looked confused. "We do?"

"Yes dear. Right now would be best."

"Oh? Oh! Of course. Tutor. Right now. We'll talk later, Mark."

They quickly walked off in the direction of the bar.

Louise laughed. "Not very subtle are they?"

"No, but perhaps the time for subtlety is over, don't you think?"

"What do you mean, Mark?"

"I love you, Louise."

Louise reddened again. "Don't be so silly!"

"I know how you feel about me. Your Dad told me. Blame him. But you know how I enjoy being with you. I loved how we could work together and have fun together. But I didn't see how you felt about me. Or us."

"He didn't tell you?"

"Yes, he did."

"The silly old fool! Wait until I..."

"Louise. Stop. You don't know how grateful I am to your Dad for telling me. I've been too daft to notice. I know you like me and I want you to know that I feel just the same."

Her face reddened again. "Oh Mark, why didn't you say something before?"

"I thought... I thought you wouldn't want me like that. That we were just good friends. I don't want us to be just friends, Louise."

Tears began to form in her eyes. "Oh Mark, I don't want that either."

So I leaned over and gave her a kiss. Her response was quite forceful!

The kiss seemed to go on forever and we had no idea that we'd been noticed. When we stopped to catch our breath, we saw the audience we'd attracted, gathered around us protectively.

"At last! Thank feck for that!" said Paddy, as unsubtle as ever.

There was a huge roar of laughter and approval.

We, apparently, were the last to know…

In Sickness and in Health?

He was cold. So cold. An iceberg sat deep inside him, despite the two duvets and the layers of clothes: t-shirt, sweatshirt, shorts, jogging pants and a pair of thick socks. His throat remained painful despite spoonfuls of linctus, cough sweets and hot drinks. He felt drained. Drained of life. Just a jumble of aching bones.

With a sigh, he pulled the bedclothes over himself again and tried to sleep. It was blissful, that slow feeling of building warmth and he relaxed. But the heat in the bed continued to grow and soon he was drenched, in a muck sweat, like he'd been toiling in the garden for hours and then been dragged through one hedge and out the other. His pounding head returned with the dizziness of falling head-first down a dark hole.

He cursed as, he threw back the bedclothes and struggled to strip the clothes off himself: the sweatshirt, the t-shirt, the shorts, jogging pants and the thick socks in order to cool himself. He lay there naked, gasping in the cool air, relieved by a moment of blessed cold. Then the chills began again.

A fit of chesty coughing took over and he spat into a tissue, throwing it on the floor. He'd long given up trying to get the tissues into the overflowing waste bin. He snorted and spat into another handkerchief, then over the side of the bed went that one too.

And so it went on, hours of polar winter alternating with the fires of hell, coughing up muck and snorting into paper tissues. He'd throw the duvet off him, he'd pull it back over himself. He'd wiggle around, trying to find any cold spot in the furnace of his bed.

He turned his pillow over and sighed at the coolness, for a moment. Then the pillow warmed and the sweats resumed. He was soaked from head to foot.

He was clearly a very sick young man.

At about 4am he was lightly dozing, but still troubled. He still moved restlessly around the bed, mumbling and sighing. His bladder woke him gradually, until there was no choice but to get up.

His feet hit the ground, but he had no strength to stand up.

"I'm gonna wet myself..." he though dully. With an almighty heave, he got himself up and stumbled to the bedroom door, hanging on to every piece of furniture he could find. He leaned on to the hallway wall to get into the bathroom and sat on the toilet to urinate. He moaned with the relief of emptying his bladder.

There was similar struggle to get up off the toilet seat. On the fourth attempt he got moving with the help of the sink, but headed for the kitchen where he grabbed a water jug.

"I'll have to pee in this…" he thought. "I'll never be able to get to the toilet again and again. I need to sleep!"

He shambled back into his room, placed the jug on the floor and got back into the Siberian bed, which fired up once more at his presence. He was soon back to shuffling and grumbling and restless avoidance of the heat. After a few hours, he fell into an exhausted sleep.

He woke around 9am and remembered, eventually, that it was a workday.

"I'll have to phone the office." But he couldn't find his phone.

He ended up on his hands and knees looking around the bedroom.

"What the hell have I done with it?"

Exhausted and desperate to go, he picked the jug off the floor and peed in it. As he placed it back on the floor it tipped over and its dark contents spilled across the carpet.

"Bloody hell!" he grumbled quietly, but had no energy to clean up the damp patch as he flopped back on the bed. The chills set in again.

He covered himself with the duvets again and tried to rest. But then his phone began to ring.

"Where...?"

He tried to trace where the ringing was coming from, but just as he began to get the phone's bearings, it stopped ringing. So he fell back on the bed once more. As he relaxed, it rang again.

"Why don't you go to hell!" he muttered listlessly. It rang long enough for him to identify the phone's location. Down the back of the chest of drawers.

"What is it doing there, for God's sake?"

Twenty minutes later he'd managed to pull the furniture back and retrieve his phone. He sat on the floor, trying to find the energy and strength to get back into his bed.

"Ah to hell with it..." he croaked as he dialled his workplace phone number.

"Hello? Hello, it's James. I'm ill. I think I've got the flu. No, it isn't 'man flu', I'm ill."

James listened impatiently as his boss lectured him about time off, illness and going straight to his doctor.

"I haven't got a doctor. Yes I know that! I've only been down here six months. I'll just have to manage. I can order food. No I don't want anyone fussing. Look I have to go…" and without waiting for a reply he disconnected the call.

He got on all fours and crawled to his bed. With a grunt he got on it and pulled the bedclothes over himself once more. He was just settled and beginning to doze when the phone rang again.

"For God's sake… hello? Who is it? Hello, Jayne. What do you want? Thanks, that's very kind, but you don't have to… OK. OK. What's the name?

'Chris'. I'll expect them in a bit. Tell them to be patient at the door, I'm slow. Yeah. Thanks. Bye."

"Chris," he repeated to himself. "Studying medicine. I suppose he might be some help..." he thought, as he napped again.

The door-bell and knocker rattle woke him. For a moment he had no idea where he was.

"Christ, just wait a minute...."

He found his shorts and t-shirt and struggled to get them on as the ringing and rattling continued.

"Why can't you frigging well wait?" he complained as he stumbled to the door.

He struggled with the locks and then opened the door suddenly. Standing there was a tall brunette in a dark blue tea dress, carrying a bag. While James was very sick, he wasn't exactly dead. Chris was extremely attractive.

"Hello, I'm Chris, Jayne's daughter? You look terrible!"

James stared at his visitor. "You're a girl..."

Chris smiled back. "Yes, last time I checked. Or a woman, to be exact. Is that a problem?"

"No, I just thought... never mind, come in."

She walked through the door and immediately took charge.

"Right. James. Back to bed for you, come on..." and she put her arm around him, guiding him back to his bedroom.

Chris wrinkled her nose at the smell of James' bedroom. "It stinks! Here, get into bed."

She pulled the covers back over him and opened the windows.

"This place needs some air and some heating. Where's the thermostat?"

"Kitchen," replied James weakly. His energy had gone again.

"I'll be right back."

He heard her walking around the kitchen and the sudden "Aha!" as the central heating boiler kicked in.

Chris came back in with her bag.

"So. You're James. I'm Chris. I'm a junior doctor at the local hospital. Mum told me you were ill and that you'd got no-one to help, so here I am."

James was too exhausted for politeness. "I don't want to be any bother to you."

"You aren't. I'd be remiss if I didn't help. Plus there's a bonus with you."

James looked confused. "What's that?"

She smirked at him. "Young. Male. A bit of alright, if you don't mind me saying. Not like my usual patients."

"I don't feel alright," he grumbled.

"I don't suppose you do. But that will change. Mum said you were handsome. So I'm very happy to make your acquaintance."

"Thanks. I think."

"Have you eaten?"

"No."

"When was the last time you ate?"

"Yesterday. Lunchtime. I think?"

"What did you eat?"

"Pizza. Delivery."

"You must be starving!"

"No. I just feel terrible."

"Thirsty?"

"Not really..."

"Let's give you a quick examination." She efficiently put a pair of latex gloves on. "Can you sit up or do you need help?"

Chris watched him as he struggled to get himself up against the headboard.

"Here. Let me help."

She grabbed him by the elbow and under his knee and almost effortlessly lifted him to a sitting position. James' head swam and he grabbed the bottom sheet in both fists to keep upright.

"A bit wobbly?" she asked.

"Definitely."

The room had begun to warm and James started to sweat again.

"Let's get your t-shirt off."

She put her hand on his forehead. "You're roasting."

Chris got a stethoscope and thermometer out of her bag.

"Pop that in your mouth. I'll have a listen to your chest. Ummm… lots of crackling. What colour is it when you cough it up?"

"Green. Sometimes yellow."

"Hmmm… chest infection."

She took the thermometer out his mouth. "38.5. You've got a fever. Any other symptoms?"

"I feel all bunged up in my throat and here..." James rubbed around his neck and up to his ears. Chris felt around the same place. "Glands swollen."

Out came more equipment as she looked in his ears. "A bit pink, but OK. What about your throat?"

"Very sore… hard to…" He was interrupted by a bout of chesty coughing. Chris held the tissues to his mouth. When he'd finished, she took a look.

"A lovely yellow… antibiotics for you. I can hear you squeak as you talk as well. Let's have a look at your throat. Hmmm… tonsils quite pink. Throat red. Put your t-shirt back on."

"So what's the verdict…?" James asked.

"I'm glad I came. You're ill enough. I'll get some antibiotics for you. But first, some food."

"I'm not hungry."

"You still need to eat."

"I don't want to."

Chris frowned. "You're still eating something. Once I find what you have in your fridge."

Chris was in the kitchen for a few minutes. James could hear cupboards and drawers being opened and closed. She came back in the room, looking annoyed.

"How on earth do you live without any food? Apart from this?" She had a packet of stale crackers in her hand.

James was embarrassed. "I usually eat out or order in, to be honest. No time for making meals and I'm not much of a cook anyway."

She let out a huff of impatience. "Typical man, living on his own. You'll have to make time. Get groceries delivered. Did it ever occur to you that you might need some food in your flat sometimes?"

James looked sheepish and kept quiet.

"Where's your keys?"

"In my trousers. Over... I don't know where they are?"

"I'll have a look around."

"I found them!" James heard Chris say as she came back into the bedroom. "Can I help myself?"

"Yeah…" he slurred. He was becoming too tired to think.

"Poor thing. You nap while I get some food and a prescription. See you later!"

James didn't even hear the front door slam, he was already fast asleep.

He woke later to the sounds and smells of cooking.

"Chris?" he yodelled uncertainly "Chris? Is that you?"

"It's me. Just let me finish this and then I'll be right in."

Five minutes later she came into his bedroom
with a tray containing a bowl of soup and some
bread and some pills. James' stomach gurgled at
the sight of the food.

"Sounds like you might be hungrier than you
think?" Chris smiled.

"I'm not hungry. Really."

"Well you have to try."

Chris sat on the side of his bed and began to feed
him with the spoon.

"I'm not a child, Chris!" James protested.

"No, but you aren't exactly yourself. Keep going,
another spoonful."

Despite his nausea, he finished the bowl of soup and half the slice of bread.

"Good. Now for pills. Antibiotics and some paracetamol."

He gulped them down with a glass of water.

"OK? Back to sleep with you, then."

Despite his objections, James was soon dozing again.

Every time he woke, she was there. Watching and helping. Cooling him with a damp cloth, soothing him with soft talk. In the middle of the night, his fever struck and he moaned and talked babble and said strange things that sometimes made Chris want to laugh, but at other times troubled her at the intensity of his illness.

At 5am, the fever broke. James settled into an easier sleep and she sat in the chair to nap.

She woke to find him trying to get up.

"I need to pee... I can't get out the bloody bed!"

"Hang on." Chris went into the kitchen and came back with a cardboard bottle.

"There. Pee in that."

James was shocked. "In front of you? I can't."

"James, you haven't got anything I haven't seen many times before. I'm a doctor, you know?"

"But... I don't see many doctors who look like you do."

She smiled in response. "Flattery and charm so soon? I'll have to keep my eye on you I think. Look. The alternative is you wet yourself. Your choice."

James grumbled as he did as he was told and soon he had filled the bottle.

"There you go. That wasn't so hard was it?" and then she blushed slightly at the unintended innuendo.

James smiled at her embarrassment. He was ill and completely exhausted, but Chris hadn't got any less attractive.

"How are you feeling?" she asked.

"Completely knackered, but not as bad as I was. Thanks to you."

"It was nothing. You just needed a bit of TLC."
Then she blushed slightly again. James looked a
sickly wreck, but he clearly was a decent looking
guy. "Definitely a bit of alright, once he's cleaned
up," she thought.

Her suspicions about her Mum's request for help
began. "Always trying to match make..."

"Time for more pills and a hot drink."

That's how it went for the next two days.
Troubled nights, regular pills, soup and hot
drinks.

By the third day of Chris' doctoring, James began
to feel more human. He certainly smelt like it.

"I'm really ripe! Can I get a shower?"

"Not just yet. I can give you a sponge bath."

"No, that's OK. I'm sure I can get to the bathroom for a quick wash."

"Not a good idea. And as your acting GP, I advise a sponge bath on the bed. I'll just get a bowl and a sponge."

"I haven't got a sponge," replied James, hoping he could get out of it.

"But I have..." smiled Chris. "You've got no excuses."

When she came back she began to bark orders.

"Right. Clothes off! And them dirty shorts. That's better. Now lie on your front."

James was still too tired and ill to argue, so he complied. He was embarrassed to be naked in front of an attractive woman like Chris, though. "Well out of my league..." he thought.

He let an involuntary moan as she went over him with the warm sponge, gently clearing off the sweat of four days. He tensed as she went over his backside.

"Just relax. It isn't the first bottom I've seen. But it's probably the nicest I've seen in a while."

James reddened again. Her touch was making him react.

"OK, time to turn over," Chris ordered.

"I'm really tired. Can't we finish this later?" said James.

"No, let's get done now, James. Come on, turn over."

"I've… I've got a bit excited. I'm sorry, I didn't mean to…"

She smiled at him. "Just turn over. I've dealt with a lot of male patients before. Young and old. It happens sometimes. Don't worry."

She rubbed his arm to help him relax, but it only made him feel worse.

"Come on, don't be shy. I'm not!" Chris encouraged. But she tried not to stare as he turned on his back. Chris grabbed the sponge and quickly went to work on James's feet and legs.

James closed his eyes and tried to think about shopping lists and football results, but his breathing quickened.

Chris cleaned his torso, noticing his muscle definition. "Not over the top like a bodybuilder, but well put together," she thought.

Despite her professional demeanour, she had begun to respond to James too.

"There. All done." she said a little shakily. "Here's a clean t-shirt and pair of shorts. I'm going to go home to get some clean clothes and take a shower. I'll see you in a few hours?"

"OK. Thanks, Chris. For everything."

She looked away from his intense gaze. "You're welcome. Try to relax."

James remained asleep when Chris returned. She watched him for a while and couldn't deny her attraction to him.

"Definitely good-looking. Seems intelligent. Sense of humour. Great body. The perfect package."

She giggled. Double-entendres seemed to come too easy with this guy.

"Mum, what have you got me into?"

She went into the kitchen and made a meal, to feed herself and James, but also as a distraction from her unruly thoughts. While it bubbled away, she came back to the bedroom.

When he awoke he smiled. "You're back. I missed you."

She tried to be business-like, but couldn't help but smile back. "How do you feel?"

"Like I've been run over by a large lorry. A few times. But much better thanks to you. And much, much better seeing you here again."

"More charm. You're on the mend then, James?"

"I like having you here, that's all. What respectable guy wouldn't?"

"Are you hungry?"

"Starving!"

"Would you like something a bit more substantial than soup?"

"A proper meal would be great."

"I have something cooking that should meet with your approval."

James tucked into her cooking with gusto.

"This is fabulous! Much better than the slop I normally eat. You can come back here again. Any time you want."

"That would be nice. But I am back on shifts in two days time."

James tried to hide his disappointment. "Oh. Then can I take you out to dinner to say thanks?"

"Of course you can. I'd be delighted."

"Anything you like. Or don't like?"

"Surprise me, James. But you need to get well first."

They continued to chat as they ate. They had similar music tastes, she laughed at his corny jokes, but she also had a great sense of humour. Dry and witty, she found humour in the darkest places.

"Graveyard humour. Anyone who works in healthcare end up with a dark sense of humour. You have to."

"I love it. There's not many women I've met like you."

"Flattery again. Keep it up, James."

When they'd finished, he had to get up to the toilet.

"Can you manage?"

"We'll soon see."

With a grunt, James got to his feet. He wavered a bit, but managed to get to the bedroom door. He leaned on the door frame to catch his breath.

"I'm so weak! What's wrong with me?"

"You've been very ill. It will take a few days for you to get your stamina back. Take it slowly. Now off to the bathroom… go on!"

He sat down on the toilet with huff of relief. He was lathered in sweat again. He got up with another grunt, washed his hands and went back to the bedroom.

"OK?" Chris asked.

"Yeah, OK."

She saw the paleness of his face and the tremor.

"You don't look OK."

She got up and helped him back to bed.

"You're hot again. Let's get you covered up."

James had a relapse in the night and his fever returned. He thrashed in the bed, shouting and incoherent, complaining of being "so cold" while burning up.

Chris grabbed her phone.

"Eric? Hi it's Chris. Yes I know I'm on leave. I'm looking after a friend of my Mum's who is sick. He's been responding well to antibiotics, but is feverish and confused again. Yes, it's a man. Yes, a young man. Does it matter what he looks like?"

Chris listened to Eric. "Yes. OK. Thanks, Eric, you're a life saver. He lives at..."

She continued to try to cool him with a damp cloth but he was still burning up. She began to be concerned and almost ran to the door, when the bell rang.

"Eric! Thank God. He's through here."

Eric, a middle-aged black guy looked at his new patient. "Good looking guy. Anything I should know?"

"No. Just tell me how we can break the fever."

"Just let me give him the once over, OK?"

Eric checked everything. Blood pressure, pulse, temperature. Everything he could think of.

"His breathing is a little bit too ragged for my liking. Let's get him on something a bit stronger.

You know the hospital is packed tonight. Everyone has this flu, so he's better at home. I've got some IVs in the car, let's get him hydrated. I doubt we'll get much down him orally. He's too agitated."

As if on cue, James began to thrash around more. "Don't leave me. Don't leave me, Chris. I don't know what I'd do... without..." and then he fell back asleep.

"He likes you, that's for sure."

"It's just a crush, Eric. You know how it is."

Eric grinned at her. "If you say so, Chris?"

She felt an irrational flash of annoyance, but smiled back.

"I have a mild sedative that will help him relax. Keep him cool and hydrated with the IV, but lots of drinks when he wakes fully. You know the drill, Chris."

"I do. Thanks for coming, Eric."

"No problem. Anything for you. And your young man."

She wanted to say, "He's not my young man", but she wasn't sure Eric would be convinced either way. So she let it go.

"See you in two day's time, Chris?"

"Of course. Thanks, Eric. Bye"

She was left alone again with James. He was calmer, but still too hot. Sighing, she went to get another bowl of water.

James woke in the morning, feeling dreadful and weak. He saw Chris was slumped in the chair, but she woke as he began to move in the bed.

"How are you feeling?"

"Absolutely dreadful. What happened?"

"You had a relapse. Very feverish. I got a colleague to come and examine you. Hence the IV in your arm."

"Wondered what that was. What's it for?"

"To keep you hydrated. You were too confused and I couldn't get you to drink. He prescribed some stronger antibiotics."

Chris gave him a hug. "I was so worried about you. Are you sure you're OK?"

He smiled faintly. "After a hug from you? I could run a marathon."

She laughed at him and let go. But she could feel how feverish he still was.

"Hot drink and some food for you, I think."

"What have I done to deserve such kindness?"

"Don't run yourself down, James. I'm happy to help you get well. After that, we'll decide how you can repay me?"

Images of how he'd like to repay Chris flashed through James' mind. He tried to put them aside. She was becoming a bit of an obsession, but one he enjoyed.

They looked each other in the eye, their faces close.

"If I wasn't so ill, I'd love to kiss her," thought James.

"If he wasn't so ill, I'd kiss him like a shot!" Chris thought in turn.

It was she who broke the spell. "You need feeding. Do you need the toilet?"

"Just to pee. I suppose it's back to cardboard bottles?"

Chris nodded at him. "You got it. Just for today, hopefully. Hang on a sec."

She returned with the bottle and left him alone as she made breakfast.

They chatted as they ate.

"You even make breakfast taste good, as much as I can taste anything at the moment. Can you give me lessons?"

"When you're better? Of course. I've got lots of things I'd like to teach you."

She looked away awkwardly. "It sounds like a sleazy come on!" she thought.

"Chris, I look forward to learning many things from you and getting to know you a lot better."

They smiled at each other. There was something forming between them and they both looked forward to wherever it led.

James napped after breakfast while Chris food shopped and got herself clean clothes. She refused James' invitation to use his shower.

"I hardly seem to see my own flat these days. A long shower in my own bathroom would be bliss."

"See you later?"

"Yes, this evening? There's a flask of soup here and a sandwich in the box. A few bottles of water which I expect you to have drunk when I get back. OK?"

"Yes, Doctor. No Doctor. Three bags full, Doctor," he rasped before a fit of coughing took over.

She smirked at him. "Serves you right. Sure you'll be OK?"

"Yes, fine. I've got your number and your Mum's. Don't worry about me."

When Chris was gone, James realised how lonely he had been before he had met her and how empty the flat felt now she'd gone.

"She's a doctor. A professional. She can't spend time mooning about you like you are about her."

He was bored on his own. There was nothing else to do but sleep.

He was awake when she returned and he couldn't hide his delight.

"Thank God. I thought I was going out my mind. Staring at these walls."

"You've got television? Or books?"

"Daytime television? I'd rather pull my fingernails out. I haven't read a book in years."

"Philistine!" she teased.

"I've had no time."

"Who do you like?"

To each other's delight, they liked the same sort of books: historical novels and crime noire.

"I'll lend you my Hilary Mantel books. That will keep you busy."

"Thanks, I've heard of her. Bring them next time if you remember?"

"You can be sure I will. Have you eaten?"

"Yeah, all the soup and most of the sandwich."

"There's some meals in the fridge, you just need to microwave it. You have cereals and snacks in the cupboard. How do you feel?"

"A bit knocked about, but getting better."

"Good. You know I can't stay tonight."

Chris saw the disappointment on his face. "I'm back at work tomorrow evening. I need a good night's sleep. Phone me if anything happens."

"I have. Don't worry. Come and see me whenever."

"Not tomorrow, the day after, about 8am. I won't be much company after a shift though."
"I'll always be happy to see you."

Chris blushed. "I've got to go."

"I wish you didn't have to."

"I feel the same. I like your company too, James."

His smile was all the response she needed. She hugged him and said her goodbyes.

When she'd gone, James felt low again.

"Better get used to it," he muttered.

He turned the light off and tried to sleep.

Small Fry

On holiday in Menorca. The narrow bay is dominated by high sandstone cliffs, with shallow, clear blue water. I can feel the beautiful hot sun on my pale white torso. It's perfect. There's no clouds in the azure sky.

I'm paddling in the water, about a hundred feet out, surrounded by tiny fish. Small fry, swimming around me.

I'm delighted like a child.

Then a rock splashes near me. I look up onto the rock and see kids. British kids.

I scowl and look heavenwards. Here comes trouble...

These kids, full of excess energy, boredom and pointless aggression are throwing rocks at the fry, trying to kill them.

One notices me glaring and grins with enthusiasm. "I nearly got one, mate!"

The moment is broken. I walk back through the surf and go as far away from these feral children as possible. A disgrace to themselves, their family and their nation. But I'm the outsider here.

I make my way to the other side of the beach and watch other people with their children: sunbathing, paddling, making sandcastles. I can tell they aren't English: they are too quiet, gentle and purposeful. There's learning, laughing and affection, with no sulking anger and bovine aggression for everyone else to suffer.

It's a place I swear to visit again. But not in school holidays...

Dope

It was my first visit to Paris and my first attempt at traveling around on my own. My mates, conservative as ever, wanted to go on a package tour to Greece, but I preferred to have a wander around and do my own thing.

Many people like to travel together. Maybe it's just one of my peculiarities. I'm restless and I like to go off as the whim takes me. When you holiday with others, you have to dance to their tune and it usually involves endless sitting in bars getting pissed. I can do that any old time!

For me, a holiday is about food, history, culture, wine and beer. Yes, the latter two can involve getting pissed, but it's a different experience.

So I got the ferry over to Calais at 1am and then the train to Paris finally arriving in 'Gare du Nord' at about 7.30am. I found the hotel, dumped my heavy ruckack and then proceeded to get completely lost in Paris.

My finest moment was asking a Parisian "Ou est Notre Dame, s'il vous plaît?" while standing right next to it. He roared laughing and I think I made his day. But at least I got there. In the end.

It's a beautiful city and I long to go back again and again. Not because of the natives, who have the haughtiness and impatience of many citizens of capital cities, but because it's got so many bits of architecture and art that speak to the soul. It's a feast for the senses and other parts that other cities cannot reach.

In the evening I met Jim, an Australian, and Kurt, who came from Germany. We shared a room at the hostel. So we went out for a meal and some of the local beer, which was quite palatable. Jim was the typical Ozzie: funny, irreverent and good humoured. I've met the occasional Australian idiot, but most, like Jim, are great fun to meet.

Kurt was a different matter. His English was very good, but he had little to say about anything. His main interest (let's not say 'obsession') came out later.

After lots of beers and an enjoyable evening, we headed back to the hostel. That's when the spliffs appeared.

I don't bother usually having a smoke myself, I prefer alcohol, but it was no bother to me. This was where Kurt's obsession came out: 'Dope'.

He started a strange monologue about "Vy I like dope", "Ver I haff smoked dope", "Vhat concerts I have been to ver the band smoke dope", "Ver I have gone to concerts ver the band smoked dope vhile I smoked dope und der whole crowd smoked dope..." and a list of bands "dat smoke dope".

He was very taken by 'The Cure' who he reckoned were prodigious dope smokers and he had seen them "vhile smoking dope vid ten thousand others smoking dope" and so on. He was also keen to let us know "vhich bands I haff yet to see to smoke dope to vhile they smoked dope, der organisers, security guards" and presumably "Onkel Tom Cobbley und alles smoke dope too."

Jim smiled indulgently while getting out his face, but Kurt continued very seriously to ramble about every permutation of "who I haff smoked dope vid, hier, der und everyver."

I think I was probably out of my mind too by the end of it. Whether that was from the fumes or from losing the will to live, I'll let you decide?

Don't Let the Baristas Grind You Down

"Four across – 'one who makes your coffee'. Any ideas?"

"Coffee maker."

"Oh, for goodness sake! Seven letters, just one word."

"Errr.."

"No, 'errr…' only has four letters."

"Does that include the little dots afterwards?"

"No, it doesn't, and anyway they're called 'full stops'."

"In America they call them 'periods'."

"Well we aren't in America, are we?"

"I was just saying…"

"Yeah alright, but can we get back to 'one who makes your coffee'?"

"Machine!"

"Yeah but it's a person, remember?"

"Where does it say it's a person?"

"It says 'one who makes coffee'."

"Well you only need one machine to make coffee, so the answer is 'machine'."

"Oh for God's sake, it says 'one who makes coffee', 'one' implies that it's a person."

"Who the heck calls themselves 'one'?"

"Umm..the Queen does."

"Well unless you're some sort of 'Queen' and you've got some sordid secret I don't know about I don't think you'll say 'one'. Or should it be 'does one have a sordid secret'?"

"I don't know why I ever ask you to help with the crossword, we always end up in bleedin' fairy land!"

"Now it's 'Queen's' and 'fairies'. I'm getting worried about you!"

"Can we please get back to the clue?"

"OK, that's fine. But if you ever want to talk to me in confidence, I'm very open-minded."

"Will you get lost? For the millionth time... 'one who makes coffee'. Not 'machine'!"

"Have you got any letters?"

"Err... hang on, second letter is an 'a'."

"Machine!"

"Would you like a punch on the nose?"

"Not particularly. Violence is the last refuge of the incompetent, you know."

"Not as incompetent as your obsession with the word 'machine'!"

"Have you got any other letters?"

"No!"

"Well what's five down?"

"Hang on... 'a mechanical device'. And don't say 'machine!'

"Motor!"

"'Motor?' That looks like it fits! Sometimes you have your uses?"

"So what have you got now for 'one who makes your coffee"

"It's something, 'a', 'r', something, something, something..."

"Can I have a look? I always get ravelled up with you and your 'something, something, something, something, something, something, something...'"

"Here..."

"Thanks. Hmmm… it's not 'machine' then?"

"Oh for a machine that would stop you repeating the same words over and over!"

"I'll record your conversations some time – then you'll know all about 'repeating', mister 'cracked record'. And anyway don't be so sensitive! It's just a crossword!"

"I am not like a cracked record!"

"You are when you get a bee in your bonnet! Like right now with this stupid crossword!"

"For the twenty millionth time, can we get back to the clue?"

"What's the clue again?"

"Can't you remember the clue? I've read it out…"

"Yeah, yeah, 'two billion times', blah, blah! Just read it out!"

"God what a... never mind! For the last time: 'one who makes your coffee'. Satisfied?"

"Barista!"

"Bah-rees-ta? It's pronounced 'bah-ris-terr'!"

"No, not a 'barrister', a 'bah-rees-ta...'"

"You're making this up."

"No I'm not."

"So what's a 'bah-rees-ta' when it's at home?"

"Someone who makes coffee in a coffee shop."

"Seriously?"

"Yes, seriously!"

"I'd got some visions of a bloke in a wig making coffee?"

"No, that's the 'barrister' in a wig. You, know, in a court?"

"I know what a 'barrister' is for God's sake!"

"Well you had no idea what a 'barista' was two minutes ago. I hope you don't get like this when you try and buy a cup of coffee?"

"I would if the so-called 'barista' was just like you."

"Well you know what they say!"

"What?"

"Don't let the baristas grind you down...!"

"Oh, God. Idiot."

When I'm Old and Lonely

Today is my birthday. I don't tell anyone.

I'm sick of them last year and their "eighty five years young'. I'm not bloody young and it isn't 'nice' and most of the time it hurts. The twinges have turned into aches and pains which go on and on.

Still. 'KBO' as Winston Churchill said: 'Keep Buggering On'. That's what I do. But the trouble is, I'm really lonely.

The carers talk to me like I'm sort of simpleton.

"Would you very much like some tea?"

"Awww look at his face..."

"Oh I don't think drinking is good for you is it, love..."

But I want to drink, eat the wrong things, smoke cigarettes and have a shag. Once a year would do! On my birthday. That would be 'nice'. I did it for forty or more years, why stop now? I don't care if it affects my health, I shall die happy.

Everyone's horrified even though they pretend it's OK. Horrified that an old man is randy. I see it in their eyes. Disgust. Disturbance. Sometimes fear. Perhaps they think I might chase them around the table a la 'Benny Hill'. Chance would be a fine thing!

No, what I want is:

1) Someone to chat to

2) Someone to actually touch and comfort and who might comfort me.

3) A kiss. Not a slobbering great snog sessions, just an affectionate kiss.

4) Slap and tickle!

5) A bit more slap and tickle!

Someone who's bothered when I'm grumpy or a bit 'off' and who takes an interest. I might be able to help them too.

But it doesn't work like that...

Yesterday I went into town and I called in to my usual cafe. There was a young bloke in my usual seat. Probably in his early thirties. I asked him if I could sit at the table.

His face was like the proverbial bulldog chewing a wasp. "If you like…." he said and then went back to tapping on his laptop.

"Lovely day," I said.

He sighed. "Yeah. Isn't it."

"Have you been here before?"

At that point he fiddled with his phone. "Sorry, I really do have to take this call."

He put his laptop in his bag and went outside. He didn't come back. I kept looking out the window to see if he was there.

After fifteen minutes there was no sign of him. So I nicked his cake. Lovely lemon drizzle cake with filling! It went down well with the tea. His loss…

I looked around. Lots of young people. Pretty young girls and teenage boys with faces like smacked arses. I smiled at one of the girls who was talking to her friends.

Her face froze. Her friends turned in their seats and gave me a dirty look. It wasn't long before they picked up their bags and were gone too.

Must have places to go. What busy lives they have!

I'm quite jealous...

The Sneak

I spotted her, a few days after I started in the job. She worked in one of the offices and had been at the company forever. I christened her 'The Sneak'.

She prowled around quietly, standing still in corridors to hear conversations in the offices. She was a ghost, unseen and unnoticed by anyone else, apart from me.

To a degree, I enjoyed it, catching her out. She'd blush and quickly try to look like she was filing away a letter or picking up invoices or whatever it was to cover her skulking. But I despised and distrusted her too. On occasion I would close the door forcefully if I was in a meeting and saw her hovering.

What was going on in her mind? What was the reason for this constant listening and intruding on the privacy of her co-workers? Why did no-one else notice?

I often wondered what she did with the information. Was it passed on in gossip or tittle-tattle? Or did she get some perverse satisfaction in knowing the secrets of the company? Did it somehow make her feel important?

I sometimes amused myself with ideas of a huge filing cabinet full of notes about who had said what to whom and when. A mammoth interlinked system about every interaction she had overheard. I'm sure she'd have done well working for MI5, the CIA or the KGB. If she could be trusted by any of them.

After a few months I began to notice her less. Occasionally I'd see a sudden movement, but I'd dismiss it. Like a chameleon, she'd faded into the background. I too had fallen under the spell.

When I left the job about a year later, she seemed quite disappointed. Her task of mapping out the entire work-life of my successor had only just begun.

A Schnortz Story

I have to talk to someone and it may as well be you. I was the one that did it. Here. I kept the box of matches. As a memento.

Do you remember when the old man died? He was a bastard! But he was good to us too. Remember Simon's wife when she got cancer? The old devil paid for the operation. He denied it, but we knew.

Then he's suddenly dead. Three years ago, almost to the day. We knew things would be hard with his idiot sons, but we had no idea how much they'd fuck it up.

It took them twelve months to destroy the company. Next thing is we're all summoned to find out we're now a subsidiary of 'Schnortz Finkelstein Schwartz'.

Some American bloke stood up telling us 'how much we were valued'. He had a tan from I don't know what planet and a dead cat on his head. But it was his teeth...

'Whited sepulchers'. It just popped in my head. Teeth like whitewashed tombstones.

Six weeks later, our senior managers disappeared. We came in Monday, they were all gone. Summoned again by the teeth bloke who went on about 'new opportunities for all'.

After a week I got hold of Pete who had managed R&D. "Sorry mate, I'm not allowed to talk to anyone. Legally bound. Don't let the grass grow under your feet..." and the line went dead.

Two months later we all had 'individualised appraisals'. I had to satisfy them that I did a good job and was value for money. An hour of humiliation. After putting me through all that, the two interviewers, Bastard One and Bastard Two said:

"Sorry Derek, we have to downsize, you'll be leaving in two weeks."

I had to sign an agreement that I wouldn't speak to anyone. Everyone else in the company got the same treatment.

So one night when the two Bastards worked late, I blocked the fire exits, switched the power off and you can guess the rest...

A Fine Bromance

I don't know what to do.

I've known Jim since we were kids, right from junior school, through secondary and then into university. Sometimes our friendship has waned, but we were as thick as thieves when we got an opportunity at school.

Right from the start, no-one could understand why I spent time with this shy and pudgy, small boy, who said little. But when he spoke he was clever and his comments were worth hearing. He was bullied, so I became his defender.

Jim makes me laugh. He's just naturally funny and quick-witted. I don't know if he completely realises it. He just sets me off with my own smart-arse comments and in the end we're a pair of idiots breathless with laughter.

I'm not sure anyone else gets it and our friendship has sometimes made others jealous.

"Is Jim your boyfriend then?"

"Where's the love of your life?"

"When are you two getting married?"

Two men being close friends? What's wrong with that? Why assume that two mates are anything more than that? And if we wanted what they suggest, what's it got to do with them? I think it's because we're so different. I'm tall and reasonably good-looking, chatty and friendly. I can charm when I make the effort. Jim is a little different…

As we went through middle school I found that girls liked me and I definitely liked girls. Jim was left behind, ignored at social events and despised by the 'popular' set. Sometimes I tried to arrange double-dates, but he was so tongue-tied and shy, the nights inevitably ended in disaster.

Jim told me stop after a while. "Go out with your latest conquest, but leave me out of it, Rich."

I felt guilty seeing him become even quieter and isolated. I know that he had a lot to offer, but no-one else seemed to be able to see it.

It was the same at university. I studied Marketing and Jim, Computer Science. I saw him less and less. His hair got longer as he retreated from the wider world into coding and algorithms. I couldn't understand a word of what he said when we met, so our friendship foundered.

We were reduced to a 'Hello' once or twice a month. My friends ribbed me about 'talking to that nerd' and I snarled my contempt for their comments.

"Jim's a nice bloke, but he'll never get a chance with tossers like you dragging him down."

It went on like this through year one and two of uni. The workload and completely different lives meant we hardly saw each other at all. I was surprised early in the last year to see him at my door.

"Hello, Rich. How are you?" he said shyly, looking at the floor.

"Jim! What are you doing here?"

"Oh, if you're too busy..."

"Don't be daft, come in. I haven't seen you in ages!"

We sat in my bedroom, drinking tea.

"What have you been doing with yourself, Jim?"

"I've mostly been looking at my final year project."

I sighed in exasperation. "Jim, I wish you'd get out more. Uni isn't just slaving in front of a computer, y'know."

Jim smiled. "I know. But we both also know that you're good at people and I'm not. That's why I came to see you."

I was curious. "So what can I do to help?"

"I've been looking at algorithms to analyse what people do and say on social media and try and tie that into mapping their social status, education levels and relative income."

I thought for a minute. "So, guess their status, education and wealth and target ads and services?"

"Precisely."

"How far along are you?"

"I've got the program nearly complete. But this is the confidential bit. I think my lecturer is a bit too keen on what his involvement has been, instead of mine."

"So he wants to take credit?"

"I think so."

"So what have you done so far?"

Jim thought for a moment. "My supervisor has seen the crudest mock-up I could get away with, while I've worked on developing the real version on my own."

"OK. What about intellectual property?"

"That's why I'm here. I can do the coding, but I haven't got the 'people' skills. I can't really trust anyone, but I trust you, Rich."

"I'm flattered, mate. But what do you want me to do?"

"I'll offer you half what its worth if you help me bring it to market."

"Is this a formal partnership or a gentleman's agreement?"

"Whatever you think is best, Rich."

"That's where you've got a problem, Jim. You shouldn't trust me either."

"But you're my friend!"

"That means nothing, Jim. I'll look into setting us up as a company. I get 30%, you get the rest."

"It should be equal shares."

"Don't be so stupid. If I'm right, we should both do well out of this. You're doing all the work, I'm just making it look pretty."

"Are you sure?"

"Absolutely, Jim. Give me a few days to sort it out. Don't tell anyone about this, OK? I mean absolutely no-one."

Jim looked troubled. "I might have said something to Craig in my flat."

"Then play dumb. Don't say any more. Nothing until we've graduated and then nothing until you finish your work."

It made life hard. We both had our studies, Jim had his 'pretend' project work and real-life development and I refined my ideas about how to market his concept. I registered 'Jimard Limited' as our company. We spent a lot of spare time together, working but also chatting.

It was like the years had rolled back. We fell into our usual roles. I haven't laughed so much since I was twelve! But then the barbs from others started again.

"What are you doing hanging around with weirdo?"

"Does he wash? I bet he stinks!"

"You seem to prefer his company to ours, Rich!"

In the end, there was only one answer I could give: "Maybe I do!"

My social life ended. Jim and I became outsiders who no-one else bothered with. I didn't give a damn, to be honest and Jim had no interest at all anyway.

Graduation was a relief! Jim got a first, despite his project producing 'a pile of crap that a ten year old could see though'. His words. He got offered a job at one of the big software companies on a decent salary. I didn't do so well.

My 2:1 was acceptable, but there were plenty of other marketing fish in the sea. There must have been thousands of us looking for jobs that would hopefully turn into a career. It didn't happen for me. There were months of unemployment, casual jobs, a brief stint at McDonalds and despairing of ever getting a well-paid job. Or any job.

I was surprised that Jim turned out to be my biggest supporter. He kept me working on ideas until I was sure it was ready. He endlessly thought of new features, but I was the one that made him stop.

"Feature creep, mate! Let's keep it simple. Then look for other stuff for version 2? Or even another product?"

"If you say so, Rich," he said, suspiciously agreeable. I knew he wasn't happy, but at least he didn't argue either. We launched it with financial help from our parents, relations and a few friends. My friends, to be honest. Then we waited. For a few months, nothing happened. Then Jim got summoned by his bosses for a roasting.

He Skyped me that night, very upset.

"They told me they won't 'tolerate an employee creating and selling products that might rival their own'."

"The bastards! What did you say?"

"I agreed to their demands."

"You did what?" I was furious at his cowardice.

He smiled. "Only until I'd had a chance to talk to you, Rich."

"Have you got any savings, Jim?"

"Oh yes! What would I spend my wages on anyway? More computer equipment?"

"Can you survive without any income for a year?"

"I think so. Enough to give you some financial security too."

So we hatched a plan. He'd go back to work, all meek and mild and I'd put an offer in to his employer to invest in our idea. If they said 'no', he'd resign as soon as possible.

I was amazed when they agreed to meet us. I turned up in my hired suit and borrowed laptop to present to senior managers. When I walked in the room, they looked distinctly hostile.

I thought, "Screw you lot!", smiled and began to talk.

I did better than I thought. The younger managers were interested and knew there was something in it for them. The older guys? They were dead set against any 'outsiders' coming in and jeopardising their cosy little set-up.

When Jim stood up to talk, they did their best to humiliate him. He stood his corner and argued to the best of his ability, but their minds were made up, probably before we walked through the door.

So the answer was 'No'. I could see that didn't go down well with the younger managers.

Jim and I drowned our sorrows in the local pub that night.

"I'm not even going to turn up tomorrow, the bashtards," hiccoughed Jim. "Tell them to..."

Before he could finish, he was violently sick down himself. We got kicked out the pub and Jim spent the rest of the night on my sofa, vomiting in a bowl.

In the morning, we were both had terrible hangovers, especially Jim. When the phone rang, I cringed at the noise.

It was one of the younger managers. He and 'several other software professionals' were willing to invest in us, 'as long as it remains confidential'. I nearly fell out my chair, hangover or not!

Six weeks later we had investors worth a quarter of a million. Suddenly the local Chamber of Commerce, after snubbing us repeatedly, offered further funding and advice. Not that we needed it, but you don't bite the hand that feeds you.

Jim happily told his employers to 'Get stuffed!' I asked him to record it on his phone, but he was so excited, he forgot!

After that it all went a bit mad. Word got around, sales started to look good and then we got an offer from several companies to buy us out, including Jim's old company which we wouldn't accept. I knew we'd got something unique and sellable and I didn't want those fossils taking it over.

A couple of years went by. We were both well-off. Not exactly multi-millionaires, but we could afford a decent house each and some swanky holidays. We spent them together. Of course the 'gay rumours' started again. We just ignored it and got on with our lives. My girlfriend, 'Isabel' liked Jim and she didn't mind him being around. Just not too much.

I was surprised when Jim said he had a date. Then a series of dates. Curious, I asked to meet the lady. And that's where I met the force of nature called 'Sasha'.

Tall, brunette and very beautiful. There wasn't a guy over fifteen in that restaurant that didn't do a double-take when they spotted her. I was immediately attracted to her too, but as she looked me up and down in return, I could see that she knew that very well.

She was sexy, desirable and completely in control of the situation and it turned out, Jim's entire life. And she wanted her hooks in me as well, I think.

Sasha sent off Jim on an errand while she talked to me. Flirtatious. Seductive. Whatever you want to call it. She was sensuous, bold and manipulative. My reaction was almost mindless. You'd understand if you met her.

"I didn't know Jim had such a handsome friend. I would have wanted... needed to meet you before."

She looked me straight in the eye and rubbed her foot up and down my calf under the table. I can't begin to tell you how tempted I was, but I thought of Jim: my friend who I love, who is more than a brother to me and the guy who had made me financially secure with a rewarding life and career.

"I just need to make a call to a supplier. Be back in a minute Sasha."

Sasha smiled, as if my rejection meant nothing. I made sure I was never alone with her again. Isabel hates her.

It was a whirlwind romance. Sasha and Jim were married six months later. Jim was deliriously happy and has never stopped talking about her since. I kept my reservations and experience with Sasha to myself.

Several years later, he's still happy. They have two beautiful children, a boy and a girl, who Jim adores. They look just like their mother, but not a bit like Jim.

Sasha is regularly spotted around the town with a succession of handsome young men.

What would happen if I told Jim? I could lose our friendship, end his marriage to Sasha (such as it is) and destroy his happiness. He'd lose access to the children he loves.

What would you do?

This story previously appeared in the 'Straight from the Heart' anthology.

Few Fond Memories

The musty smell. The endless tick-tock of the large clock. The antique furniture. Antique minds dulled by time, limited imagination and petulance. Peter is five years old and there's running to be done, 'tick 'a nick' to be played, swings to be swung on and war games to be fought. Laughter, silliness, delight and everything else that just happens when you're five.

But he's there at his Grandmother's house in silence for hours half-listening to the grown-ups talk about the things they did last time they were here and the time before that. Peter remembers, you see, even if the grown-ups don't.

She's always 'Grandmother', not like the other one who smiles at him and says silly rhymes and tickles him and feeds him cake and tells wonderful stories and he loves Grandma more than he can bear. Almost as much as he loves his Mummy. He knows they are both the same. And he is too.

The monotony is broken now and again by the cheep of Grandmother's budgie, 'Peter'. The human Peter hates that little bird: it does nothing but stare, peck aimlessly and chirp. It's not very exciting. He shares its name. The human Peter, five years old, is already embarrassed about being named after a budgie.

In the years to come Peter would be endlessly teased about his name by his older brothers and sisters. There's nothing wrong with it, but who wants to be named after a useless bird that does nothing? Peter already understands now that it was his Daddy's idea and that's when he begins to comprehend, in a small way, how stupid and insensitive his father really is.

"Speak up, your Grandmother can't hear you!" snarls Daddy. Peter knows his Daddy is angry. He's always angry. Visiting Grandmother makes him worse. Perhaps he's bored too, but Peter knows better than to ask. So he sits in silence and tries not to shuffle, but fails.

"Will you keep still!" snaps Grandmother at him. Peter hears the same tone of voice. Daddy and Grandmother shout at him just the same. He doesn't really like either of them.

Mummy tries to defend Peter. "He's only a small child, Florence. He can't sit like a statue?"

"Then if he can't behave like a civilised boy, send him outside!" retorts Grandmother.

When Peter thinks of the old woman in later life, he smiles. She was trying to punish him, but it was the only gift she would ever give him apart from her contempt: out in the garden! No grown-ups and their boring talk!

To run, jump up and down the concrete steps, to roll down the lawn, to laugh and cry and battle his imaginary friends and enemies. To live in the moment.

To be absolutely free...

Because I'm Weak...

My dearest Vanessa,

By the time you read this, I'll be long gone. You said it a few months ago: 'You're weak'.

It's true. That's why I'm running away. Because I'm weak.

When you were expecting the baby, we were full of excitement, but that changed at the three-month scan. We were told that Olivia would be severely disabled and a poor chance of survival. Less than 20%. You wanted to give her every chance, but I had my doubts. The doctors warned us of the possibility of multiple operations, a limited lifespan, blindness, deafness, physical disability and behavioural problems. They suggested a termination. You forcefully argued for Olivia's life and eventually, reluctantly, I agreed.

Because I'm weak.

Now she is two months old. Five operations, endless hours in critical care and yes, she is blind, deaf, physically disabled and has a limited life expectancy. Everything we were warned about has come true.

Olivia will never have a normal life. She will always be dependent: for physical care, eating, toileting, and endless doctor and hospital appointments. Twenty four hour care a day, every day, until she dies. We will have no lives of our own. I cannot face that prospect. Because I'm weak.

She will never smile, take her first steps, and have temper tantrums, go to school, become a teenage rebel, break my heart, grow up, become accomplished, fall in love and have children of her own. A bit like the beautiful young woman I met and fell in love with a decade ago. You. I cannot face that barren future. Because I'm weak.

I cannot bear to see you become harder and more desperate as you argue and cajole and battle for every last little piece of help. Where you angrily turn on everyone: friend or foe, in frustration and anger. I've seen it in you already in just two months. You will not be the women I loved, eagerly married and wanted to share my life with.

When our peers glow with pride about their children's talents, hobbies and accomplishments, Olivia will remain the same. She will grow and become so much more unmanageable. The cute baby will turn into a less cute toddler and into a lifelong commitment for you and me. I cannot bear that burden. Because I'm weak.

When she is a young adult, she will need even more specialised care that you and I will have to fight for it. I have no heart for that fight. Because I'm weak.

We will break our backs, dragging her from bed to toilet, to wheelchair, to seat. Lifting, rearranging, strapping her down, wiping her bottom and giving the most intimate of care. I have no stomach for this. Because I'm weak.

I warned you. The doctors warned you. But your heart, your spirit, your natural desire to protect your child drove you on against my advice, pleas and even when I begged you at the end. You were too strong. So I am leaving you. Because I'm weak.

The house is yours. Half our savings are yours. I will pay for Olivia's maintenance. That is where my interest has to end. I cannot bear to see what happens to you and to her now or in the future. Because I'm weak.

Love and regrets,

Charles.

A Random Act of Kindness

George worked hard in the week, night shifts and sometimes alternating day work. He was always over-tired and frequently bad-tempered, which eventually led to divorce.

His children took their mother's side and he rarely saw them.

George threw himself into work. It was all he had. At the weekend he saw no-one and he, being a middle-aged man, was usually ignored by everybody. The sum of human contact most Saturday's consisted of, "Would you like a carrier bag?" or for variety, "Can I have a carrier bag?"

Then it was back to his rented flat with lots of cans of 'Old Speckled Hen'.

Sundays were spent hungover, in bed. Until one weekend...

It was the usual Saturday shop. Booze, pizza, takeaway meals. For some reason that particular week, George noticed the bunches of flowers, at half-price near the tills. He admired them for a few minutes and thought about buying some, but as usual his thoughts turned darker.

When he got out the shop, he was followed out by an old lady who called after him.

"Darling! Darling!" She spoke in a cut-glass posh accent. Curious, he stopped and turned.

She smiled at him. "I saw you looking at the flowers. You always look so unhappy, but for a moment I saw how happy they made you. So, here. Have a bunch on me."

George was flabbergasted and tried to refuse, but he was a little shocked to be noticed by anyone. So he took the flowers and an attempt at a smile was made.

"Thank you," George said to her, in a quiet voice.

"You're welcome darling!" she replied. "I must be off. Have a lovely weekend!"

All the way home, passers-by saw George carrying the flowers and they smiled at him. While George on his own was sullen and lonely, the flowers gave strangers the opportunity to interact with him.

He gave a rusty grimace back. By the time he got home, he was quite happy.

The next week he bought a bunch of flowers for himself.

The Stink

Jeff woke from a troubled sleep. It had been
hard to settle with everything going on in the
night. Mostly silence. A deafening silence. Like a
graveyard. Literally.

Occasionally he'd hear drunken shouting in the
distance and the smash of glass, followed by
hysterical laughter. He was glad he'd moved into
the back bedroom, so no lights could be seen. It
used to be his Mum and Dad's. He sometimes
smelled his Mum's favourite perfume in the
room and it upset him.

There's a different smell this morning. It makes
him want to gag and run away. It unsettles him
and makes him fearful. He's tried to not think
about it, but 'The Stink', as he's started to call it
is getting stronger by the day. Jeff knows it
means danger and disease.

With a grunt he got himself out of bed, fully dressed. He had an inkling that sooner or later the drunks shouting in the distance might notice he was there and he'd have to get moving quickly. Two sharp chefs knives lay on the floor next to his bed.

He went down the stairs, quietly, listening for any noises. Cleo rubbed around his legs, greeting him with a 'meow' and then headed for the front door. She wanted to go out, but he didn't dare let her. She'd crapped all over the carpet in the living room even though he'd put a tray in there for her. He decided to leave it.

Jeff went into the kitchen and boiled some water using the gas cylinder. He scolded himself for trying to turn on the electric kettle. "Fat lot of good electric kettles are now!"

He daren't set a fire as it might attract attention.

Ten minutes later he had a strong mug of tea, but 'The Stink' still pervaded the kitchen. As he opened the back door, the full stench of it hit him. It was like walking into a brick wall. Any idea of eating breakfast ended as he recoiled from the stench.

"I think I need to go…" he mumbled to himself. "But where…?"

He closed the door again and sprayed air freshener everywhere. It masked the smell for a short while. He walked into the dining room, grabbed his pad of paper and began to write lists.

Most of it was about food. There was another list about medication and antibiotics and plasters and anything he might need for an accident. Who was going to help him but himself?

He had another list for booze. He liked a drink and he didn't see why that should stop, but he was wary. He'd seen some people in the street, clearly out their minds and it frightened him. He didn't want to end up like that. A drink for his nerves would be nice though. Jeff knew he was in shock. Everything seemed distant and had no impact on him, apart from 'The Stink' which was a constant reminder. The events of the last few weeks would shock anyone. He knew that.

"Something to deal with later. With a bottle of brandy. Or maybe not. Worry about that at the time..."

He drove to the nearest car showroom. "Something big? A 4x4 would do? Maybe a van? Yeah, lots of room for supplies."

Two hours later, he was at his local ASDA. The doors were slightly open, so he knew that other people had been about. He checked to make sure he had the knives with him. He filled the van with cans: soup, stew, coffee, tinned vegetables, anything that would keep for a few years. Everything perishable was already going off: the fruit and veg rotting in the supermarket aisles.

He'd just finished packing everything away in the van, when he saw the kids. About twenty of them, early teens. He had an immediate instinct they were trouble. Suddenly, they were throwing stones at him and shouting abuse.

"This is our place! Fuck off mate!"

Jeff drove away at speed, hearing the crash of stones and bricks against the sides of his van. He knew he would not be able to visit the supermarket again.

"Is it all going to be like this?"

Back in the dining room, he looked at his lists. Tomorrow, drugs. Then he'd have to go. 'The Stink' had got worse as the day warmed. He grabbed his father's road atlas. Well out of date, but there was no Google Maps or Internet access now.

"Somewhere far from towns? But I need to get supplies? A farm? What the hell do I know about farming? But I'm going to have to learn..."

He knew that built-up areas would soon be too dangerous: cholera, typhoid and other diseases would soon be rampant.

"Cornwall might be good?" He noticed how he had started talking to himself out loud. Apart from the kids in the morning and the drunks at night, he hadn't heard a human voice in weeks. Just his own.

"Cornwall it is. Climate is good. Small towns. Bristol and Exeter are near. It's rural. Don't know where else to go?"

The next two days were busy with adding anything else he needed from the lists. He spent an hour trying to get Cleo into a carrier. She made life difficult for him and his hands were covered in scratches, but he couldn't bear to be parted from her.

"You're the only thing I've got left, a bloody nasty cat!"

Cleo hissed her resentment at the unfair treatment. Jeff carried her to the van and put her on the passenger seat. 'The Stink' made him want to be sick. He went back through the house, into the back garden and walked up to the fire pit that he'd built on the lawn. He'd lost count of the days since he set it alight.

"Goodbye, Mum. Goodbye Dad."

Before he could get too upset, he walked back through the house and pulled the front door shut. He didn't bother locking it.

Five minutes later he was on the road heading south, his vision blurred at times by tears.

No Particular Place to Go

Sitting alone in her studio flat, in Clapham on a Friday night. She didn't know anyone and there was no particular place to go, either.

Margaret threw down her book in frustration. Three months of work and weekends reading books, eating chocolates and bottles of red had taken their toll. She was bored and lonely.

"What am I going to do about it?" she thought.

"Classes?" She liked evening classes, but rarely liked the people. They all seemed either terrified to speak or so over-confident and convinced of their genius it was ridiculous.

"Gym?" Full of narcissists, male and female, admiring themselves in the weight room mirrors or copping off with each other. Not that she'd mind a bit of copping off, but Margaret felt she still had some standards.

"Not that desperate. Not yet, anyway."

"Sports?" God, she hated sports and sports fans and sports venues with a passion. Freezing to death while everyone else cheered on. "No, thank you!"

"Bars?" Being chatted up by another little cockerel with his even smaller cockerel had got so tedious. She'd tried a drink in her local, but there was always some male on the prowl. Some old enough to be her granddad!

"Dating agency?" She snorted with laughter into her latest glass of wine. She knew people who'd done it and it had worked for them, but she didn't like the idea herself.

So she settled back into the chair, picked up her latest novel and took another swig of red wine.

"After the next chapter, a few more chocolates..." She hated the idea that reading had become dominated by eating and drinking, but it kept her going.

On the Monday, she was almost relieved to get to her office, dressed in her best working suit. On the way to her desk, she bumped into a fit-looking guy. Tall. Jet black hair. A tan, Well-built. She thought he'd do very nicely. It also turned out to be his first day.

"Hello, I'm Dave. And I'm very lost," he said, looking at her with his mesmerising green eyes. She enthusiastically introduced herself and took him along to HR. Suddenly, her working week was looking up!

"I'm free at lunch if you'd like me to show you around?" Margaret asked.

He smiled, showing perfect white teeth. "I'd like that."

Every day after that they met for lunch and chatted. He was musical and played the guitar. So did she. A week later, he invited her out for dinner.

Antisocial Media

Matt picked Georgina at her front door. She looked beautiful, dressed in a clingy and revealing black dress. A little black number that he could hardly take his eyes off.

Attraction was entirely replaced by lust, he admitted to himself.

"Just one minute, Matt," she said. "I just need to text Mum to say you've arrived."

"That's fine," he replied. "She does know who I am, doesn't she?"

Georgina grinned. "Oh, yes! I've told her all about you!"

Matt's thoughts flitted back to their last night. Georgina had seemed well-pleased too. "I hope she didn't tell her Mum all about that...?"

During the taxi to the restaurant, Georgina updated Facebook, sent three tweets and took a picture for...? She wouldn't say, as she was too busy looking at her Instagram updates.

Not once did she speak to him. No:

"How are you, Matt?"

"You look smart!"

"I love you."

"I want to shag you senseless like we did the first time we met..."

"Did you see the Financial Times article on the shares crisis...?"

"I'm looking forward to the meal..."

There was complete silence for the rest of the taxi journey and it continued as they sat at their table. Georgina took Snapchat pictures of the menu and sent several more messages. Her tongue poked slightly out the corner of her mouth as she concentrated. Matt thought it would be endearing if it was focused more on him and not on her smartphone.

After the starter and the main was ordered, the phone calls started.

"Hi babe," she answered. "I'm with Matt. Yes I did! No, he's not my 'latest conquest'. It's Matt! I'm sure I did?

"Maybe I announced it on Twitter?"

He tried to get her attention, smiling and trying to get into her field of vision, but Georgina continued to focus on phone calls, texting, social media or other apps he didn't know about.

He tried a polite splutter, but that too was ignored, until he looked on the verge of a major coughing fit. The waiter came over and offered Matt some water. Still Georgina focused on her phone.

It wasn't until he waved his hand directly in front of her face that she responded.

It was fierce!

"What do you want to do that for? Wavin' your bleedin' 'and in my face? 'Aven't you got any fackin' manners? If I told my bruvvers about what you just did, they'd kick the shit outta you! Fackin' idiot!"

Matt couldn't fail to notice how her accent and manner had changed. Gone was the well-modulated accent. Instead he was face to face with what sounded like a cockney fishwife, out to give him hell!

"Well? Ain't you got manners or what?"

Matt took his own phone out his pocket in desperation and answered it.

"Hello? Joe? What's up? Oh no! Where is she? OK, I'll be there as soon as possible."

He looked up at Georgina. "Sorry darling, my mother has had a fall and been rushed to hospital. I must go."

Georgina's face softened. "Oh babe, you must! Hope she's OK. Give her my love!"

Her accent had softened and returned to 'posh' and her farewell was affectionate and caring.

Of course there'd been no phone call at all. He never answered her calls, texts and emails ever again. Especially when she called him a '****' repeatedly on Facebook, Twitter and LinkedIn. And Instagram. And Snapchat.

And WhatsApp.

A Stranger Inhabits

Eddie watched her from a distance, warily. The old lady in the bed stared into nothing. There was no movement, no concentration and no awareness of the ward around her: the nurses chatting, the occasional moan from another patient and the rattle of the trolley carrying newspapers, chocolate and sweets.

He was too frightened to approach her.

The nurse saw him dithering and came over smiling. She was Caribbean, smiling and happy, in contrast to his mood and reluctance.

"What's up darlin'?" she asked.

"I came to see that lady over there," Eddie replied, pointing at the old woman's bed.

"Enid? Are you family or friend?"

Eddie scowled. "I don't think I'm anything now."

The nurse frowned too. "What do you mean?"

Summoning up his courage, Eddie looked back at the bed and then turned to face the nurse again.

"Can you come with me? I don't want to frighten her."

"Of course I can, love. Come on." The nurse motioned for him to follow.

The old lady didn't respond in any way as they approached her.

"Enid. Enid! You have a visitor," the nurse said loudly.

There was no response.

The nurse spoke again, putting her hand on Enid's shoulder. "Enid! Enid! You have a visitor. A lovely young man! Do you know who he is?"

Enid looked up, firstly at the nurse. There was a spark of recognition and then a smile.

"There you go. That lovely smile of yours, Enid."

The nurse pointed at Eddie. "Now, who is this man who has come to see you?"

Enid looked over. There was no sign of recognition, no lovely smile. Just indifference and a hint of fear.

"What's your name, love?" asked the nurse.

"Eddie," he replied.

The nurse raised her voice again. "This is Eddie, Enid!"

The fear in Enid's face grew. The fear of the stranger or a perception that the man was some sort of danger. The old woman shrank into the bed, as if trying to get away.

"She doesn't know you, love. It happens a lot when they get to this stage."

Eddie tried to smile back at the nurse. "It's OK, I've been expecting this for a long time. Thanks for trying, though. I don't want to keep bothering her and you."

The nurse smiled too. "You're welcome, darlin'. Shout if you need anything."

Eddie turned back to Enid, who continued to stare back, as if he were a threat. He smiled faintly at her and put the flowers he was holding on the bed. The old woman's eyes briefly looked at the bouquet, but immediately went back to Eddie, full of distrust.

She had always loved flowers. Now she was a stranger. So was he.

As he walked away he softly said to her, "Goodbye, Mum."

There was no reason to go back.

The Finer Things in Life

George sipped again from the glass of port. "Good stuff," he mumbled to himself.

It had been a gift from some MP at some party a few months ago. "MP for…?" He couldn't remember. Another oily politician wanting a favour. It had been another one of those events where he had to press the flesh, smile the smile and pretend to know and like his guests.

"What a lot of shit they all are…" he grumbled to himself. "I think I preferred it dealing with the market traders down the Estate."

'The Estate' was where he came from. Fifty-five years ago. All hidden away by a fictional life. No more 'Georgie Ellis', living hugger-mugger with his Mum and six siblings in a council flat in Romford. Now he was 'George Trusley-Elwin', property developer, financial advisor and a bit of a playboy. His name was in the newspapers often, accompanied by one supermodel or another.

"Life is sweet," he thought to himself, but he longed for the days when he was free to wander the streets, get in a bit of bother, make a quick deal for some dodgy gear and then flog it on the Saturday market. It was a bit wild, often full of violence, but the desire for a bit of a punch-up sometimes consumed him. But this life, full of meetings and charm and schmoozing with the idle rich imprisoned him. He hated it, but he didn't know how to get out of it, or even if he wanted to.

George tried to restrict his violence to the gym. He'd apologised to Freddie, his regular sparring partner after what happened last week. "I got a bit carried away Fred, sorry about that."

Freddie, a successful amateur boxer, looked worried but agreed to carry on. George despised that fear. Freddie would have to go. George needed a younger guy to box with, who was full of piss and vinegar and attitude, giving as good as he got. That was the challenge.

"My only challenge these days…"

Tonight he was alone. Last night it was 'Aubrey', "Some fuckin' Yankee tart," he chuckled to himself. "With a copyright name, for fuck's sake!"

She bored him within minutes, but he had to go through the motions: charming, seducing and finally getting her into bed. She was alright, but everything she said or did, came out of a low grade porn film. The gasps, the sighs, the encouraging words, everything was just fakery.

He had responded with his own particular brand of fraud and promised to catch up with her later in the week. An air-kiss and she was gone in the morning. He'd spent the rest of the day reading up on what was going on in his company. He like to keep an eye on what was what, especially after what his previous accountants tried to do to him. Sooner or later they might bob up out of the Thames?

"Maybe I need a holiday?" He'd got the place in the Caribbean.

"Nah! Somewhere away from Richard. Showing off, as usual. Own island and all that bollocks." He spent the rest of the evening thinking and swigging the port.

"I think it's time for a change..."

Something Has Changed

Harry remembers it decades later and it comes back to haunt him now and then. It's so long ago...

He no longer experiences that vivid shock and bewilderment he then felt as a small boy. Now it fills him with a bleak sadness: a life unlived, a future cut short and the agony of parents losing a child that he can well understand.

His first experience of seeing a dead person happened when he was eight.

It was a typical Spring Saturday when everyone wakes up from seasonal torpor and they start to clean, paint, decorate, sort out their gardens and start to live again after a harsh winter. Everyone is out sweeping, mowing, scrubbing and cutting things up. April has arrived and the urge to be outdoors is very strong.

Harry's Dad virtually lives in the garden once it's light in the evenings, and there he stays: digging, scowling and throwing things around. Harry knows better than to disturb Dad when he's gardening.

Mum's Spring obsession turns to cooking: pies, cakes and trifles: the trifles that makes Harry's mouth water when he thinks of them. As far as Harry's concerned his Mum is the best cook in the world, especially puddings and cakes.

Mum has sent him to buy some custard powder at the small shop down the road, opposite the post office. Harry doesn't go in there often and he doesn't like the man behind the counter. This shopkeeper doesn't like children at all, or so Harry thinks.

"What can I get the young gentleman?" he thunders.

He's so enormous and so loud! Harry doesn't trust the jolliness in the voice. He wants to run away, but he knows he needs custard powder. Otherwise there will be no trifle.

"Well? Cat got your tongue? What do you want?" asks the shopkeeper again, all pretence of a smile gone.

"Custard," replies Harry.

With a grunt the man goes and gets custard from the shelf behind him.

"That'll be thirty-seven pence."

Harry fumbles with the money Mum has given him, disturbed by the man and his glaring. He promises to himself he'll never come back.

"Oh give it here!"

The shopkeeper snatches the coins from Harry's hands and throws the money in the till, thrusting the tin of custard at Harry.

"There! Anything else?"

"No… no thank you," stutters Harry.

He gets out of the shop as quickly as he can, running up the road with the tin in his hand. He suddenly realises that the shopkeeper has not given him any change. What will Mum say?

Back a home, she berates him. "I wanted custard powder! I told you what I wanted. This is tinned custard! Why don't you ever listen? And you paid too much! Where's the change?"

"He didn't give me any change…" replies Harry, becoming more fearful by the minute. An angry Dad is a temporary inconvenience but an angry Mum means no trifle, cake, pies or anything nice in the whole world.

"What do you mean, no change?"

"I didn't know…" says Harry helplessly.

"You go back right now. You get the custard powder I asked for and you get the change. I gave you forty pence, I expect change when you come back. Off you go!"

Harry tries to object but Mum is adamant. An adamant Mum is impossible to sway, but going back to the shop and facing the shopkeeper is equally as frightening.

"I don't like him."

"Like who?"

"The man at the shop."

Mum grits her teeth and her lips go thin. "I don't care who he is or what you think of him. You shouldn't let anyone diddle you out of money. Do I have to go down there with you?"

The prospect of Mum shouting at the man in the shop is even worse. She's done it before. Everyone would see. He'd be mortified. Everyone at school would know. All the local kids would hear. Their parents would laugh at him behind his back. He'd do anything to avoid that mockery.

Even go back and face the man on his own and get his money back.

Harry trudges back to the shop, walking slower and slower. He spots Philip, one of the older boys from school who waves and smiles as he pedals past on his bike, a bucket precariously hanging from one handlebar.

Harry likes Philip. Everyone at school likes Philip. He's sporty and clever but he's nice. Always smiling, always cheerful and always kind. He doesn't bully anyone like many of the older boys do. Like Hugh.

Harry tries not to think about Hugh and what happens on Monday. Every Monday.

When he gets into the shop, the shopkeeper is still there, behind the counter.

"Oh it's you again. What do you want this time?"

Harry is silent and can't think what to say.

"I haven't got all day to wait for you, I've got other customers to deal with, you know?"

Harry looks around the shop and suddenly feels a flash of anger. There is no-one else there. The man has diddled him of money. He didn't give Harry the right custard. Harry will not have his well-deserved trifle.

It all comes out in a rush. "You gave me the wrong custard an' never gave me change an' you tol' me the wrong price an' my Mum is angry an' she says she'll come down an' sort you out if you don't give me what she wants."

The man looks at him with a smirk. "Oh yeah? What's Mummy's name then?"

"Mrs Price."

The condescending grin fades from the shopkeepers face as he recognises the name. He mutters under his breath, as he fetches custard powder and gets the right money out the till.

"There. Now clear off! Next time ask your mother to give you a list!"

Harry flees the shop as fast as he can, tin of custard powder in his hand. As he walks out the door he sees…

It will stay with him the rest of his life.

It's Philip, lying on the floor, his legs still wrapped around his bike and his bucket still on the handlebar. But he's still. So still. His usually animated face is pale and his unblinking eyes are open, staring right at Harry.

There's a big arc of something purple-red going out from the top of Philip's head across to the other side of the road. It looks like a raspberry lolly that's half melted: liquid and solid bits.

Harry doesn't really understand, but he sees the adults clustered around and their looks, some near to tears.

That shocks him most of all.

Philip still doesn't move.

Harry sprints up the hill to home as fast as his eight year old legs can carry him and he bangs the knocker and rings the bell, quite overwhelmed by what he's seen.

Mum answers the door. "Whatever is the matter?" she asks as he babbles and the tears begin to flow. Hot. Endless. Tears.

Harry is in a total panic and he struggles to tell Mum about Philip. To get words out that makes sense.

She takes him into the front room, sits him on her lap even though he's a bit big for that now. Mum hugs him until he calms down, whispering over and over to him,

"You'll be fine. Don't worry Harry, you'll be alright.'

When his crying has subsided a bit she goes into the kitchen and reappears with a mug of tea, hot and sweet. He sits there quietly drinking it and

Mum perches on the armrest, her arm around him, consoling him. Comforting him.

Harry stays quiet for the rest of the day even when she puts a bowl of trifle in front of him a few hours later.

He eats it to please her, but he doesn't really want it.

Something has changed.

The Old Bugger Turned Ninety Last Week…

He sat there in his chair. Look at him. Sitting in that bloody chair. Face like a smacked arse. It would curdle milk. All ninety years of him, pickled in hate and this, his worst day of the year. Today he has to deal with people he can barely tolerate and sometimes loathes.

The feeling is entirely mutual.

He's ninety years old and he hates fuss and attention, except when he can't get it. So he didn't get any. That would have made him extra surly, but he doesn't know what day it is anyway.

His strength has gone, he can't see very well, he can't hear either. It's a torment to try and talk to him as he's so frustrated. Just like the rest of his life. Frustration and anger and tantrums.

Repetition after repetition after repetition gets tedious. So we mostly sit in silence or make sotto voce comments to each other. You'll have to forgive us, it's the only entertainment we have.

So he gets a birthday card. He can just about tolerate them. Strangely enough, he likes funny ones: the man with no discernible sense of humour likes funny birthday cards. It must come out of him when he doesn't notice or when he lets his guard down. There might be a cheery man somewhere inside, but we will never know.

I don't think he's smiled in about twenty years and it must be forty since anyone has ever seen him laugh.

We all bring him bags of sweets. He's very grateful for about three milliseconds. Then it's back to sour looks but his gob is crammed with them. Like a geriatric cement mixer, the confection goes around and around his mouth. At least it shuts him up.

We all turned up. Unusual. Even more strange, we didn't fall out. It's almost like we sense that something is changing. His force, that will, that strength and that dominance has come to an end. There's no need to squabble when the source of it has no more influence.

He's just a very old man, who smells of piss a bit, gets cranky, rants about someone who upset him seventy years ago and then falls asleep. Laughable really.

It's almost encouraging when he snarls at his carer. "Will you stop bloody fussing?"

She's a saint. Smiles. Fluffs his cushion and comes back ten minutes later with a mug of tea, which he accepts with a grunt.

We manage an hour then get out with sighs of relief. Then we laugh.

"Same time next year then?"

Two weeks later we get phone calls. "He's dying," the voice says.

"Let me know when he's dead," I think, but I make suitable sympathetic clucking noises and make vague promises about when I will visit.

I put the phone down, feeling quite excited.

Soon, we will be free…

A Dissenting Voice

Tom was in the pub having a well-deserved beer (or five) after a bit of a shitty day. Everyone had been an utter bastard: surly customers, late deliveries and that new kid in the office needed a punch on the nose. Beer was the obvious answer. As he chugged down his first beer, he spotted Moz, one of his old cronies, over in the corner, staring at the floor.

This was not the Moz that Tom usually saw: he seemed quiet and isolated.

Moz: one of those 'geezers'. All East End bluff, but behind it, decent and honest. If he liked you, you were fine. If not, it was probably best you went and lived somewhere else. A long way away. Tom had known Moz for years and they'd always got on.

So he decided to go over and have a chat. Later he wished he hadn't.

"Alright, Moz?"

Moz looked up and grimaced. "Yeah, alright, I suppose."

"You don't look like it, mate."

Moz gave a sigh. "I'm just a bit pissed off with everything."

Tom laughed. "What? Everything?"

"Yeah. Everythin'. The whole lot. Every-fuckin'-thing."

"You can't be."

"Well I am."

"It can't all that bad, Moz?"

"It is, mate."

Tom shook his head. "There's got to be something to look forward to."

"Well there ain't."

Tom stopped a moment, desperate to think of what to say, but Moz beat him to it.

"I fuckin' hate Michael Jackson."

"Why?"

"'es a pedo, ain't 'e? But they still keep goin' on about 'ow wonderful he was."

"That was never proved you know."

"Yeah, but he paid everyone off didn't 'e?"

"But that doesn't mean…"

"The only thing about 'im that made me laugh is when the Fulham fans were singin' 'I'm Forever Blowin' Bubbles' when that loony Al-Fayed owned Fulham and he invited Jackson to a match. "

Tom couldn't help but laugh again. "Suppose so. But it can't be just Michael Jackson."

"No. I'm fucked off with 'earing constantly about gay rights, transgender agony, people with Post Traumatic Stress Disorder from a friggin' paper cut and celebrities tellin' us how to live. Why can they keep their bleedin' boat races shut?"

"Come on Moz, there's nothin' wrong with gay rights."

Moz glared back at Tom. "Did I say there was? I don't care what people do, I just don't to 'ear about it every day some fuckwit bleating on about 'my gay journey' or some other thing to make us feel sorry for them. I do feel sorry for people, but I've 'ad it up to 'ere with 'earin' about it."

"But Moz… people need to know."

"I don't want to know."

"Why not?"

"Because I've got the gas and 'lectric bill, me mortgage, feedin' the kids, not murderin' the missus and puttin' up with that bastard Lewis at work every day. Not to mention the 'ouse needs paintin', everything gets dearer by the day and me Mum is as mad as a box of frogs. In care.

Thinks I'm me grandad and I have to call 'er 'Florence'."

Tom sighed. "I can see where that would get you down a bit, but you aren't the only one, mate."

Moz interrupted. "The telly's shit, the news is all about fuckin' Brexit, the Middle East or that orange arsehole in America. Or the fuckin' Royals. I might want to know what's going on in South Africa or South America or anything but Arab civil wars or that dickhead causin' trouble. That Trump, what a twat he is."

"But these are important issues, Moz, you can't pretend they don't matter."

Moz glared again. "I do care! But not day in day out, every fuckin' day the same crap on the news, the same wanky sitcoms, the dramas about middle-class knobs I don't care about. And

that Poldark bloke. All them women all gettin'
into a right two and eight about him takin' his kit
off."

Tom pulled his face. "Yeah, I know. Glenda keeps
drooling."

"Mine does too. Fed up with 'Poldark this,
Poldark that. 'Why ain't you more like that Aiden
wotsisname, a bit more sexy', she keeps sayin'."

Tom wanted to laugh. Moz, with a bald head,
beer belly and a too tight England shirt was not
exactly anyone's idea of 'sexy'.

"Maybe you could try to woo her, Moz."

Moz put his head in his hands. "Fuckin 'ell, not
you too. She's been readin' all them wimmin's
mags. "'Ow to 'ave an orgasm if your bloke is

useless in the sack'. 'How to become a lesbian if your man is a bit limp'. Makes me sick."

"Women have needs too, mate."

"I know that! I just… I just can't do it like I did."

"Like what?"

Moz's face reddened. "When we shacked up, we were like fuckin' rabbits. We 'ad such a laugh. I loved 'er to bits. Now I can't, you know… do it. She's so randy, I 'alf expect 'er to run off wiv the 'Ouse 'Old Cavalry. It's demeaning."

He took another swig of his lager. "Nobody gives a fuck about what I want. All I get is 'me, me, me, me…' To honest, mate, I wish they'd all fuck off and die."

"Come on, you don't really mean that Moz?"

Moz paused in thought. "No, I don't suppose I do. Apart from Lewis."

Then he grinned. "I'd dance on the wanker's grave. I'd even do a fuckin' jig!"

Moz's enthusiasm quickly waned and his head dropped back in his hands.

Tom was stumped. He didn't know what he could do to help. "Want another pint?" he asked.

Moz lifted his head.

"Yeah. Go on then. I'll 'ave another Stella, mate."

Nothing to Fear but...

In the end, it's all about nothing and all about everything and it's been going on the last few days but also forever.

What am I talking about?

It's the smothering mother and father and simultaneously having to be 'Mummy's Girl' as well as 'Daddy's Girl' and being a disappointment and a failure at both. For my Mother it was not being sporty enough, not in the Lacrosse team, not beautiful enough. For my Dad, it came down to a 'lack of intellect', 'not being clever enough' at school, at learning and not knowing what I wanted to do. I worked hard and got B grades and B+ on occasion.

It was never enough. So they decided, when everyone else went off to university that I should pay for my lacking: my 'laziness', my 'daydreaming' and my 'intellectual deficits'.

Only a Russell Group university was good enough for the family. They would not contribute to a place at a 'lower' university for me and I had no means of doing it myself, or the confidence to find out how. Dad would not let me sign on as he thought it 'a badge of shame and failure'. So I still had no money and not a bit of independence.

It was off to find a job, with no help, no encouragement from anyone and as a result, no success. I froze when asked what I was good at or what my ambitions were because I didn't know. How can you ever know when everyone else makes decisions for you?

It made the home life worse when my father decided he would 'no longer tolerate a daughter of mine sponging of the family'. It was 'a job or out the door'.

If this was going to suddenly make me apply for the next executive job at a major corporation, they were mistaken. My parents' fantasies about what could be achieved 'with good hard work' met the reality of unemployment and competition for every job. I ended up applying for anything and everything.

Down at the local fish and chop shop, there was a job going. So I applied and got it.

Of course, the parents were horrified and hounded me for weeks to give it up, but I wouldn't. I was quiet and shy and never wanted an argument, but I became angry at their complaints and insinuations. As far as they were concerned, working at a chip shop was akin to prostitution!

I got to know some of the other girls working there: sometimes evening shifts and sometimes lunchtimes. Some of them were dog rough! But they treated me well and I got invited to nights out. They sensed I was unhappy and got it out of me.

"Your Mum and Dad sound like total wankers, love."

"If you want to get out I'll help you get somewhere."

It was nice to have some friends and people who took an interest in me, but I still longed for something else: a bit of class, a chance to learn, being with people who liked to think. There was no chance of that working evening in a chip shop and being at home with the now loathed parents.

It all came to a head at home when I'd sneaked out for a night with my workmates. I'd got more than a bit tipsy and I had to endure the lectures from both parents as well as a pounding head and the strong desire to be sick the next day.

Hangover or not, it all came out: in a screaming voice I told them both exactly what I thought of them, with their faux poshness and their stupid middle-class pretensions and that I'd rather have been raised by a colony of rats than them. 'Rats have more humanity' I shrieked before I went out the front door, tears running down my face.

I never went back. One of the girls at work offered me her sofa for the night which turned into two weeks. They all rallied round at work, offering me a place to stay: two days here, a night there, until I got the offer to share in a bedsit.

It was a bit of a comedown! It was grubby and some of the other people in the house were well weird, but I was determined to never go back to 'Them'.

That's what my parents had become. 'Him', 'Her' and 'Them'.

A week later my father confronted in front of everyone at the chip show, demanding I 'come home' and 'stop behaving like a silly little girl'. I'll never forget the look on his face for the rest of my life. I relish it. It keeps me warm at night.

I'd learnt some choice language from my customers and the best response I could come up with was:

"Fuck off, you old twat!"

I'll never forget my utter delight at how his face went white and then red and how he angrily tried to drag me over the counter. It became legendary in the fish and chip shop and the story has been retold over and over, becoming more exaggerated each time.

He wasn't so cocky when the owner called the police and dear old Dad was arrested.

How impotent and ineffective and useless he was when faced by a woman young enough to be his daughter, but wearing a police uniform. How pathetic he was. How eager to please. How apologetic he could be when faced with someone he thought more powerful than himself.

That was the last I ever saw of him. I explained to the uniformed woman what he was like and she urged me to press charges. I couldn't be bothered. I wanted to be free of Him and Her and Them and Their Lives.

Two years later I'm working at Wilko's, still in the bedsit and got a boyfriend. He's gentle and laid-back. Wants to be a musician. I don't think it will come to anything but he's good company and I think I love him. A bit.

I've got a life of my own. I'm starting a part-time degree next year.

I still have times when I'm frightened and unsure. I still doubt. I still think I'm not good enough. I still have days and weeks when I'm down. Like now.

But like I said to Him, fuck off if you want to make me frighten or doubt myself.

Every man and every woman who I meet that tries to drag me down. Just fuck off.

Time Jumpers Revisited

Oh God. That kid is staring at me. Kid? He's well into his twenties. But he's got 'the look'.

Now the girl with him? She can stare at me any time. She looks fed up. What's she doing with a fanboy like him?

Oh no, he's summoning up the courage to talk to me… oh for God's sake! Time to put on 'the face'. It's another acting job, so get on with it. Never get paid for it, though. Here he comes…

"Excuse me, but are you Cyborg XP3?" he says, shyly.

I smile back. "Yes, that's me. 'May the Gods of Cyberton Cast their Gaze Upon you!'"

He breaks into a big smile. "Oh wow! It really is you! I loved you in 'Time Jumpers'. What are you doing now?"

"Oh. This and that. Big role in Casualty, then some theatre work."

"Great! We never see you at conventions, though?"

"Oh, you know how it is. Too busy rehearsing and on the stage. An actor's life is never dull!"

The geek's lady friend looks over and I give my most charming smile. "And who is your delightful companion?"

"Oh that's Chelsea. She doesn't like science fiction very much."

I try to not let my disappointment show. I could do with some female company and she'd fit the bill...

"Each to his or her own... errr... I'm afraid I don't know your name."

"Tim. Tim Piggs."

"Hello Tim. So nice to have fans of 'Time Jumpers' after all these years."

"I love it! Do you remember the episode where you went through a space portal and ended up..."

I zone out. How the hell do these people expect me to remember a job from twenty years ago? Fortunately Tim knows the episode much better than I do.

"And then you ended up in this parallel universe…"

I smile and nod to encourage. I look over at Chelsea and she rolls her eyes. I smile at her and she returns the smile. Bingo! This old devil's still got charm.

"And then you had to be rescued by using a special Time Jumper that was built by the 'Old One's'…" Tim rambles on.

"And all you could say at the end was 'It is most agreeable to be reunited with the appropriate quantum resonance'. It still makes me laugh!"

By this time Chelsea has made her way over and is sitting next to me. She's intrigued. Good. Time to up the charm.

I interrupt Tim. "So this is Chelsea? I'm most gratified to meet such a beautiful lady…"

I kiss her hand. Her face reddens slightly. Gotcha!

Tim is oblivious to the interaction. He's still blathering on about parallel universes, quantum fissures and something about a reunion?

"You haven't been invited?" he asks.

"Oh I'm sure the invite will come at some stage. I may be busy of course."

"But it's tomorrow! The reunion is tomorrow!" says Tim.

"Ah! In rep you see. No time for nostalgia. Give my regards to my fellow 'Time Jumpers'. Especially Lady Matrix!"

"Oh. That's a shame."

"Yes, it is. But now I must be off! Dress rehearsals in thirty minutes!"

I get up and shake Tim's hand firmly and then Chelsea's more gently with a little stroke of my thumb. She reddens again. Interested? Worth a try.

"Chelsea. If you don't mind me asking, would you be free some time to help me with my lines? It's always a passion to work with others. Genuine human contact is such a help to an actor. The rewards are always... pleasurable."

She looks at me and then away, flustered and then at Tim. "I'm... I'm not sure... Could I...?"

He's delighted. "Go for it, Chelsea! Wow! My girlfriend working with Cyborg XP3! It would be so cool!"

"Here's my card, Chelsea. I look forward to getting to know you better."

I squeeze her hand again and another little stroke of the thumb.

Then I'm gone, a little spring in my step.

"You old fraud!" I laugh to myself.

Building a Civilisation

He sat there in the chair, shaking and disorientated. How long had he been playing?

It didn't matter. He was 'King Ralph' of the English and he was conquering everyone before him. It was the Aztecs next...

His head swam a bit. He tried to shake it off but the blurred vision continued. He could barely see the computer screen.

"Need a break... I'm so tired... just one more turn..."

He sat closer to the monitor. "That's better. Now if I could just discover armour, then I could defeat them much easier. Have I got enough Gold? Yeah... let's lower the... the taxes"

His legs had long gone to sleep and the pins and needles in them had faded away gradually. He was too occupied by the game anyway. He had to win! He had to get higher points than the last game! He had to beat Kev who always seemed to do better!

One turn led to another and another as more hours passed by. He discovered tanks and he'd conquered the Aztecs. "But what next?" he muttered.

"Rockets. I have to get rockets. Then I can build the 'Apollo Program' and then it's satellites and a spaceship! I can kick everyone's ass after that. What's my points now? Not bad. I'll be able to stick it to Kev on Monday? Or is it Tuesday tomorrow?"

He had no idea what day it was or time of day. The curtains had remained closed. He'd ignored the hunger pangs, his full bladder, the aching back, the numb buttocks and his stone cold feet. It had all merged into a general ache which he ignored for the sake of winning the game with maximum points.

He carried on playing, although his hands trembled badly.

Three days of solid Civilisation gaming was too much, even for a healthy young man, but he was far from healthy. He was already obese from a sedentary life, mostly sitting down playing computer games. The blood clot that had formed in his leg moved around his body and up to his brain.

He was dead before his head hit the keyboard, accidentally declaring war on the Babylonians.

No-one noticed his absence for over a week.

Full Moon

I was a bit wobbly after several pints of beer as I walked home from the pub. It was two o'clock in the morning and the full moon was high and bright in the sky, the dark clouds repelled by its intense light. It was awe-inspiring and magnificent. I stood there for fifteen minutes watching the spectacle above me.

It was wonderful and disturbing and humbling and frightening and exciting to see, this huge portal in the heavens, full of power. I could believe in gods and mysterious forces reaching out to influence me and the world around me.

Just for a moment.

Gender Fluid Cuisine

Jill and Cressida were arguing at the bar. Yet again. As usual, it was about food.

They'd been coming into the pub for about nine months. Most of the men nodded politely but having the two women there made them uneasy.

"Maybe they're lesbians?" asked Tom.

"That Cressida must be. Look at that 'air. Buzz-cut. Blokey clothes."

"She might be explorin' her gender fluidity, mate," replied Eric.

"Her gender what?" Tom was outraged.

"It's all that girls who are boys who like boys to be girls stuff."

"Ain't that a Blur song?"

"Yeah it is."

"I used to like Blur, but not any more. That Damien Allbran bloke is a complete knob."

"Why?"

"A load of arty-farty bollocks. What a plank. He should've stuck to writin' pop songs, not that thing where he pretends to be another band. Chimpanzees, or whatever it was. Load of bollocks anyway."

"It wasn't Chimpanzees."

"Well what was it, then?"

"I haven't got a clue. Who cares anyway, want another Stella?"

"Yeah, go on, mate."

While Tom waited, he watched the two women still arguing.

Cressida was waving her arms about in an alarming way. She was an attractive looking women with blue eyes and light-brown hairs, but the tatts and the piercings and the near-skinhead made her look hard as nails. That was what especially made the men in the pub wary of her.

Jill looked a bit more conventional. She was dark-haired, nearly black, with red highlights. She was pointing her finger and jabbing at Cressida as they argued.

"I told you, Cress, it's coriander you want, not turmeric. It nearly made me sick, it was so spicy. Next time try and read the instructions. Every time you make it up, it's a disaster, darling."

"But it's so boring, Jamie Oliver, his books. I hate the blandness. I like to jazz things up."

"Jazz up is great, darling, but not blow up. I don't know why you like his books anyway. He's like some over-matey adolescent, 'wiv 'is cockerny fakery. Like an overenthusiastic embryo, ruining our meals."

Jill frowned. "I know, sweetie, but he's advertised as some sort of cookery guru. That's why I bought the book in the first place."

"I wish you'd throw it away. Then we can eat without fear."

"That would be marvellous, but I've already cooked and frozen his vegan jerk rice."

"Jerk rice? What on earth's that?"

"I have no idea. It sounded like a good idea at the time. He's the only jerk of course."

"How many meals, Cressida?"

"Stop calling me 'Cressida' like you're my mother. I hate it!"

"Sorry. How many meals, Cress?"

Cressida looked at the floor, guilt written all over her face. "About twelve."

"Twelve? We have to eat twelve of the embryo's jerk rice rubbish?"

"I'm sorry, Jill. I got the measurements wrong."

"Again! If you didn't make us live in such clutter, you might be able to find a measuring jug."

"I know. But you know what it's been like…"

"Yes! Yes! The book! The book! The book! You're going to tell me how much agony it is, then burst into tears. "

Cressida looked furious. "What a nasty bitch you are! I should have stayed with Roger."

"Why don't you go back to him, then?"

"Because I like being with you. I love you. Not him."

Jill couldn't help the grin that appeared.

Cressida tried to keep the scowl on her face, but she couldn't quite either. "See? You know it. Nasty bitch! Always criticising my cooking! I've a good mind to make you do it from now on."

Jill looked alarmed. "What, cooking? Oh no! No! No! No...!"

"Why not?"

"Remember the last time I tried to make toast? The fire alarm going off?"

Cressida snorted with laughter. "Then it's Jamie Oliver or fire alarms. You choose?"

When Tom got back to his seat, Eric was watching the two women intently.

"Told you they were lezzies, mate."

The Cat's Bejewelled Bottom

"The poor bastard, look at him…"

Tom and Eric were watching Phil, sitting at the bar, looking miserable and well into his fourth pint of lager.

"Why does he put up with it?" said Eric.

"Dunno. Loves her. And those bloody daughters of his. That's what he told me. But it all sounds like a nightmare."

"I thought they were alright, his missus and those girls of his?"

"They were, Eric, but they all seem to go a bit mad at twelve or thirteen. Moody, snappy. He gets no peace. Jessica's got just as snappy too.

So he comes in here and pours it down him three or four nights a week. Then wobbles off home."

"So what do they say to him?"

Tom gave a little sigh. "It's the usual teenager stuff. Everything he says to them is greeted with eye rolling, or strops. Apart from that, all they do is stick their heads in their bloody phones."

Eric pulled his face. "Mine was a bit like that, but she was alright some of the time. What do they do with those phones? All day, looking and fiddling with 'em."

"It's called 'Angry Birds'," replied Tom."It's a game. I don't know what you do: catch 'em, shoot 'em, but that's what Phil's daughters do. All the time. Apart from snarling at him or their Mum."

"Talking about angry birds, how's your Mercedes?"

"The same," replied Tom, looking morose.

Eric grinned back. "Still demanding whatever takes her fancy?"

"Oh yes! Last year it was a horse, this year she wanted driving lessons. At fifteen! Then she wanted to bring over some spotty little oik and then stay all day in her bedroom. With the door closed! She screeched like a bleedin' banshee when I said 'No'."

"So what's she want this time?"

Tom took a big swig of his beer. "I tell you, mate, the world's gone mad. Guess what she wants for her birthday?"

"Not another friggin' puppy?" replied Eric.

Tom looked down at the softly snoring Labrador under the table and nudged the dog with his foot.

"I think this one is enough, don't you? No, she's decided she's offended by the cat's bottom."

Eric let out a snort of laughter. "You what?"

"She thinks seeing the cat wandering around tail up minding its own business is disgusting."

Eric scowled in puzzlement. "But that's what cat's do? And they sit there, leg up licking it when I'm trying to have me tea."

"I know. Marty, the little bastard used to do it too. I'm sure it's on purpose."

"So how are you going to solve the problems of the world concerning the cat's arsehole then, Tom?"

"She wants some sort of jewelled thingy to cover it up."

Eric snorted again with laughter and his beer came out his mouth and up his nose. In between laughing and coughing, he gasped,

"You... you bastard! I'll get you for that."

Tom laughed back. "No, it's true. She seen it on that Facebook thing. It 'angs off the cat's tail and covers up its arse."

"Are you serious? Come on, it's got to be a joke?"

"No, straight up. She showed me the website. 'In seven different colours of your choice, from amethyst to racy red, all to cover up your favourite feline's brown star'. Obviously I'm making the last bit up."

"Marty would have gone mental if you'd tried to 'ang anything off his tail. He'd probably have your leg off at the knee. Fierce little bugger, I hated him sometimes. But he didn't like anyone messin' him about."

"A king of cats, your Marty was, Eric. His own boss. Mercedes' soft little bugger will put up with anything. 'Phoebe' she calls it. Phoebe wants a boot up her jewelled arse if you ask me. Not even allowed to go out. Sits there meowing all the time for food or a fuss. Muggins here has to clean up when it craps."

"Tell you what, though, Tom, I've got a great idea for something that might cover up your dog's bollocks."

"Would it stop you talking it too, mate?"

"That's another great idea, Tom. We'd be minted!"

They sat in silence for a few minutes, watching Phil's unsteady attempt to get off his bar stool.

"Fancy another pint, mate?"

Pop Goes the Cap

This was the day I sort of went a bit mad. Like when you're a kid with a bottle of pop when you shake it and shake it and shake it until the cap can't withstand the pressure and off it goes. The fizzy drink goes everywhere and it's all wasted, but like the kid you are, you're pleased. Delighted in fact.

I'm now supposed to show remorse. Sorrow for what I did. The truth is, I am pleased. I am delighted. The pop is out the bottle and it can never go back.

I've lived this life: go to school, go to church. Obey. Don't cause a fuss. Don't be the slowest or the stupidest, just sort of keep yourself under the radar. Don't attract attention and whatever happens, don't bring embarrassment to your family or the wider tribe.

And whatever you do, don't attract the attentions of the police. "It won't go well for you, lad," my mother and father always said.

So. Ordinary. Boring. Sensible job. Office-based. Married at twenty-five. Two children who I don't understand at all, but I do try to love them.

Wife? I feel nothing for her now and she feels nothing for me, but we're safe together. Comfortable. Convenient.

My son is a bit of a high-flier. I've tried to keep his feet on the ground, but he's bold. Daring. He wants to see and try everything. I've tried telling him to set his sights a little lower, but he just ignores me. I'm pleased when he does well, but it worries me as well. The attention he seeks and gets. Good and bad.

He's in heaven at sixteen because he's sporty and quite clever. He's a good-looking boy and he revels in the attention he gets from girls. It makes some of the other boys quite jealous. I didn't realise how bad it had got until last week.

The police called. The boy is in hospital. Someone stamped on his head. Spleen ruptured. Bones broken. Nose pulped. My handsome, golden son is a lump of battered meat.

Numb. Numb. Numb. More numb. Even when my wife shrieks in hysteria when she sees the boy: all wires and pumps and the hissing and beeping and the heartbeat, slowly jumping on a screen.

The chaplain turns up and prays for my son. The wife gets comfort from it. I am polite. My daughter is kept away. At thirteen she is too young. She is with my wife's sister.

He stays the same for a week. Then he dies.

The two brothers that did it are arrested and there's some sort of trial. They are poor, stupid, and aggressive and have nothing to offer the world. Just more violence and chaos. They'll spawn more brats just the same.

They laugh at us when they are declared innocent: them, their parents, their friends and their family. A great mass of impudent and stupid scum, all heading to the pub to celebrate.

It's relatively easy to find out where they live. I'm patient.

So this is what I do. The internet is great. A crude but functional explosive device. Crammed with whatever filth I can find. Razor blades. Excrement. Medical waste. Rotten meat. Bleach. All mixed like a devil's brew. All on a timer.

When the police came and arrested me my wife cried. I was taken aback. I didn't think she cared at all. Bless her, she does.

I deny nothing. Those boys and their family took my son away. Took his life. Those of them that have survived will have a hellish life: amputations, infections, trauma and years of counselling. Years of not being able to hurt anyone else.

Good.

They will never be able to do to anyone else what they did to my boy. My golden, happy, sporty, quite clever boy, who they hated and in their jealousy, killed.

Whatever punishment you think will fit my crime is irrelevant. Do you really expect me to care?

Old-Me and Young-Me: an argument

Old-Me sometimes meets up with Young-Me and they have a chat. Well, to be honest, it's usually an argument. An inter-generational tiff of the strangest kind. Fortunately Middle-Me (that me) mostly gets ignored.

I feel fortunate.

It seems to follow a pattern. The old man gets angry and then furious and the young man gets defensive. Then the old man tries reason, which gets him nowhere and then he gets into a sweary strop.

It always starts the same way. Old-Me start getting nostalgic. "Why, I remember…"

Young-Me rolls his eyes and shuffles his feet, fed up with Grandad blathering on and there's a flicker of panic when he realises this is how he's going to end up.

"Listen when I'm talking to you...!"

Old-Me starts with his usual regrets. "You're angry and pathetic and you let other people run your life. Your mother, your father with all their nonsense. Don't spend decades before you realise they both talked shit."

Young-Me rolls his eyes. "You sound just like Mum and Dad. Both of them. Simultaneously. It's more than twice as annoying."

The older man huffs in annoyance, then starts to laugh. "Well I am your mother and father. So are you. You just haven't had the chance to get as annoying like they were to me. Like they are to you right now."

"They are."

"They are. They were. And they will be. Forever and ever, Amen! So don't pay attention to them if they are that annoying."

"You did."

The old man sighs. "I did. What a knob I was."

"Hey, I'm no knob!" protests the younger man.

"But you are. All that energy, all that good-looks, all that potential and you don't know your arse from your elbow."

"You're all arse," retorts Young-Me.

Old-Me's eyes twinkle. "So you can understand! Well done, my boy. I am an exquisite arse. A vintage arse with lots of time to appreciate how much arsery is better for me. The rest of the world can go fuck itself."

"You swear more," says Young-Me. "I try not to swear."

"Ah get lost! I remember. You were all pious but behind it all, you swore like a trooper. And don't forget all those naughty thoughts you have about Helen."

Old-Me sighs again. "The beautiful Helen, with her great tits and a lovely bottom. Never mind all that religious bollocks, go and chat to her. Go and chat her up if you dare?"

Young-Me reddens in embarrassed. "I would never think about Helen that way..."

"Oh yes you do... all that wanking on the quiet. I remember all that furtive stuff and that stash of magazine under the carpet. Better for you if you go and chat to her, chat her up, make her think you care. All you want is a shag after all?"

"That's not true, it's not right for me to think about her like that."

"You naïve little bugger. I am you. I was you. I'm just warning you that life goes quickly. I spent years pining after women without the testicular fortitude to talk to them. I got married late, we never had any kids but I absolutely adored my wife."

"Was it Helen?" asks Young-Me.

Older-Me chuckles. "Helen? She was just some spotty girl with no brains in comparison. The one I loved, the one I married was so superior: she laughed, she cried, she was intelligent, she was arty, she earned far more than me. She was the most beautiful thing in my life."

Young-Me looks puzzled. "Why did she like you, then?"

"I don't know, kid. She just did. Someone up their likes me. Well, once in a lifetime."

"So are you still married?"

The old man looked sad. "No. She died. I don't really want to talk about it."

"Have you got anyone? Any friends?"

Old-Me shook his head. "Not anymore. It doesn't really matter. In the end there's only me. Looking at the state of me now, that's not guaranteed for much longer. No more me, shortly."

The young man looks puzzled. "How much will I remember of all this?"

"Not much. It's like that crappy science fiction you still read, all metaphysical la-di-da nonsense. Think about it like it's a vivid dream. Try not to ignore it, like I did. Like I probably will, you dozy little git."

Young-Me gets angry. "You're still an arsehole, you nasty old bugger. How much of this do you remember?"

"I remember it as it happens. Don't expect me to explain all this. I haven't really got a clue. Don't spend all the time trying to figure it all out neither."

"So what am I supposed to do?"

"Find people who you can love. Not just to have sex with. People that you can talk to, people you want to share with, people you want to be with. It's not Helen. She's smashing looking, but she's as thick as double-ditch. You need people you can communicate with."

"What am I going to do with my life? Haven't you got any more to tell me?"

Old-Me paused in thought. "Yes. Go forth and multiply, in every sense of the word, you self-righteous little prig. Go and live a little instead of being some sort of lukewarm, eunuch wannabe. Careers are a load of rubbish. It's people and places and dogs and cats and everyone you meet. The rest means nothing."

Then the old devil pointed straight at me. "And don't be like that dickhead, sitting there listening and not being involved. He sits and writes, but he doesn't join in. What sort of life is that, then?"

38490550R00215

Printed in Poland
by Amazon Fulfillment
Poland Sp. z o.o., Wrocław